JONATHAN EMS

THE Outside World

BOOK ONE: WEREWOLVES OF LANDFALL

Pineapple Hell Publishing

ISBN: 978-1-7379143-1-0

Cover design by MiblArt

*For anyone
who has ever used
"weird"
as a compliment.*

PROLOGUE

The room was lit only with candles and smoldering cigarette butts, as was befitting any respectable ceremonial sanctum whereupon great and powerful beings practiced the dark arts and sometimes played cards.

The circular room had been made with the greatest care and attention to detail that money could buy. Fabulous motifs, ancient symbols, and forgotten languages trailed alongside detailed depictions of early man's rise up the food chain. The great beasts of the Earth locked in a violent struggle against the upstart humans played out in fractal progressions and forbidden geometries around the room.

The center of the room was occupied by a heptagonal slab of stone that acted as both a sacrificial altar and conference table. It, as well as the seven stone chairs that surrounded it, rose up from the floor like cursed appendages that wailed in visual pain at their dark intentions.

The artisan who had carved the entire room from a single block of volcanic stone had worked tirelessly, etching each detail by hand. It had taken him more than a decade to complete, and he'd taken his own life upon its completion, honored to be the first to spill his blood on his masters' shiny new sacrificial table. Since then, only the Seven Fathers and their Favored Son knew the room even existed.

Cartright's eyesight was starting to fail him, but he didn't like bringing his reading glasses into the ceremonial chamber. It was of little consequence for someone like Stimms to wear glasses; he'd been wearing glasses his whole life. But for Cartright, putting on his glasses felt like a surrender to his advancing age. It put him in a bad mood, and his cohorts had already lectured him about bringing a negative vibe to the sacrificial table.

"Just tell me what it says," Cartright said, handing the files back to Hollander.

Hollander sighed and opened the files. "One of our acquisition assets in Landfall has come to the attention of law enforcement," he said, looking over the reports.

There was an uncomfortable murmur among The Fathers.

"How the hell did that happen?" Shumacher sneered.

"That is unknown at the moment," Hollander said, still flipping through the pages of the report. "It seems there was some sort of civil case that prompted attention. The FBI is already sending an agent to investigate."

"Which asset are we talking about here?" Wilcox asked.

Hollander leafed through the pages. What was happening was at the forefront of the report. Who it was happening to was less of a concern and was buried a few pages in.

"It hasn't been connected yet," Hollander said, "but it looks like this has to do with Arthur Remus."

All seven hooded figures seated around the table

murmured in concern as a goat bled quietly into the seven-pointed star carved into the top of the table.

"Can this be contained?" Cartright asked.

"Doubtful," Hollander said. "Lawyers and reporters are all over it. It would make more sense to sever our connection to Remus."

"We have a lot of assets in Landfall," Ogden piped in.

"Ogden's right," Cartright said. "It's in our best interest to protect Remus."

"Within reason," Wilcox said. "We can't risk exposure just for a few soldiers."

"Not just 'a few soldiers,'" Hollander corrected. "Once The Seal is broken, they're supposed to be our elite guard. Not to mention the damage that could come if any of our other assets lost faith in our protection."

"We have a lot of assets in Landfall," Ogden repeated, louder this time.

"Yes, thank you, Ogden," Cartright barked back. "Perhaps an audit is in order."

"Do we have time for that?" Johnson asked. "The FBI has already taken notice, and there's only so much influence we have over them."

"I have confidence in Our Son's abilities," Cartright said. "He'll have little trouble hindering the progress of a single agent as he conducts his own investigation."

The seven men murmured amongst themselves again as the goat took its final breath.

"All opposed," Hollander announced, officially, "speak now."

None of the Seven Fathers spoke up.

"It's settled, then," Cartright said. "A full risk assessment of Remus and his...pets? Whatever you want to call them.

Our Son will have full authority in Our Name to mitigate any damage as he sees fit."

"Perhaps," Johnson said, "there should be *some* restrictions. You know how he likes to impress us."

Cartright nodded. "No executions or sacrifices without our blessing," he said.

The other six figures nodded in approval.

"Make it official," Cartright nodded to Hollander.

"The Fathers have spoken," Hollander announced, ceremoniously.

"Our will be done," the others responded.

Over two-thousand miles away, Special Agent Carl Abrams' plane touched down in Landfall.

CHAPTER ONE
WELCOME TO LANDFALL

C arl arrived in Landfall with little fanfare, just how he liked it. He knew the press was already onto the case, and would be looking for any sort of government official they could harass for more details. But he'd become an expert at not looking like a government official.

While his colleagues mostly relied on their image of authority to bully their way through a case, Carl had long since learned that his small stature and bookish frame only hurt his efforts to come off as intimidating. He found that by taking advantage of others' underestimations of him was his best weapon.

After disembarking his plane, Carl walked right past every reporter that was camped out on the other side of the security checkpoint. They were there looking for an FBI agent, not an accountant in an overcoat. He was practically invisible as he shuffled past them and climbed into a taxi.

The taxi ride to Landfall Police HQ was a menagerie of every sense Carl had remembered about the place. The city rolled by in all the colors, sights, and smells that had assaulted his senses the first two times he'd been there. The whole city was like an over-confident film student's final project come to life. Each successive building looked like an argument between the architects, and the streets were laid out like someone was trying to make a point about existential nihilism. This was a city built by, and for, people with a bone to pick with "the establishment."

While the taxi was stopped at an intersection, Carl watched two men with matching pink mohawks barge out of a vegan sushi storefront and immediately draw swords on each other. Carl had to remind himself that his authority here was limited to the case he'd been assigned, and wasn't at liberty to intervene. He'd just have to let the taxi carry him away and hope they'd work it out on their own. After all, they had waited til they were outside before they drew the swords, so hopefully that meant the dispute wasn't that heated.

"First time in Landfall?" The cabbie asked him. He had gone almost a full 20 minutes before speaking up, which was the longest Carl had ever experienced with any cab driver in America.

"Third," Carl responded. "Still not used to it."

"I've lived here for thirty years," the cabbie said. "I don't think you ever get used to it."

"You must see all kinds as a cab driver," Carl said.

"Better believe it, pal," the cabbie said. "Every day it's something new. Like, for example, your name wouldn't happen to be Carl, would it?"

Carl blinked. "Yeah," he said. "it is. Why?"

The cabbie didn't say anything at first. As the cab rolled to the next intersection, he stopped at the red light then turned to face Carl.

"Are you serious?" the cabbie said. "Your name is really Carl?"

"It's a common enough name," Carl said. "Why is this weird?"

"Can I see some ID?" the cabbie said.

Carl frowned, but complied. Even though he wasn't officially questioning this cabbie about anything, it was standard procedure to present your credentials when asked. Carl held his badge up for the cabbie to see.

"Shit," the cabbie said. "You're a Fed."

"Care to tell me what this is all about?" Carl said, putting his badge away.

The cabbie took a breath, seemingly embarrassed by what he was about to say.

"Yesterday," he began, "this kid jumps into my cab. He hands me a twenty dollar bill, and this phone number."

The cabby produced a folded slip of paper that looked like it had been torn from the corner of a larger sheet of paper.

"He said," the cabby continued, "'When Carl gets in your cab tomorrow, tell him to call me.' Then he left. I didn't even drive him anywhere."

Carl took the slip of paper from the cabby. "That is pretty weird," he said.

"Am I being pranked, or something?" the cabby asked.

"I should be asking you that," Carl said.

The light turned green, and the cab started moving forward as Carl and the cabby sat in silence for a moment. Carl looked at the phone number written on the slip of paper. It was a local area code, but that didn't mean much these days.

"He didn't say his name?" Carl asked.

"Nope," the cabby said.

"Can you describe him?" Carl asked.

"I don't know," the cabby squirmed. "Just a normal looking kid. 'Hair-colored hair,' as my daughter would say."

The cab pulled up to Police HQ and the cabby printed out the receipt for Carl.

"You really got no idea?" the cabby asked.

"I know as much as you do," Carl said. "Maybe I'm the wrong Carl. Like I said, it's a common enough name."

"Brother," the cabby said, shaking his head, "I'd be willing to bet a day's pay that it's for you."

"What makes you say that?" Carl asked.

"Welcome to Landfall," the cabby said, and drove away.

* * *

"You want my people to run this down for you?" Lt. Franklin Burgess asked, looking at the scrap of paper with the phone number scrawled on it. "Dust it for prints? Maybe call in a handwriting expert?"

"Your enthusiasm is breathtaking," Carl responded, sardonically. "But yeah, if you wouldn't mind."

"I'll get right on it," the lieutenant said, dropping the slip of paper onto his desk, where it immediately blended in with all of the other sheets of paper that had gathered there. "Shall we get down to business?"

The two of them in the lieutenant's office, which somehow managed to feel windowless, even though the entire back wall had a fifth-story view of the downtown street. Carl supposed that had to do with the dismal weather. The whole city felt windowless.

4

Carl shrugged. "It's your house," he said.

Burgess opened the file folder in front of him.

"Special Agent Carl Abrams," Burgess read aloud. "Masters in Criminal Psychology, Masters in Chemistry, PhD in Economics."

The lieutenant stopped and glanced up at Carl.

"Economics?" he said.

"Money is the root of all evil," Carl said with a shrug.

"Uh huh," Burgess responded, and turned his attention back to the file. "You were on the Domestic Terrorism Task Force?"

"I specialized in identifying credible threats," Carl confirmed.

"Why'd you leave?" Burgess asked. He threw the question out casually enough. In the past, people would ask with a hint of careful suspicion behind it. Some of them wondered if he had pissed off a superior. Others already knew the answer, but they were hoping the political pundits were wrong and that Carl would say so. But Lt. Burgess seemed to be genuinely curious.

"Budget cuts," Carl said.

"Budget cuts?"

Carl nodded.

"Why do I get the feeling there's more to it than that?" Burgess pressed.

"Because there is," Carl sighed, "but I didn't come here to talk politics."

Burgess nodded, closed the file folder, and handed a second one to Carl.

Carl already knew the basics of the case; eight families had gotten DNA confirmation that the babies they had brought home from the hospital and had been raising for the last several months were in no way genetically related to either parent. In the process of filing civil complaints with the hospitals they had given birth in, they'd come to discover that a) between the eight of them, they had given birth at three different hospitals, b) the births of the babies in question were up to five months apart, and c) none of them had each others' baby.

All that was bad enough until the news picked up the story. It wasn't just that these eight families had swapped babies by accident. It was that the eight children they'd been raising were not related to anyone. They'd come from seemingly nowhere, and the children whose names they were using were nowhere to be found.

"We figure we've got about a week before this turns totally batshit on us," Burgess said.

"How do you figure?" Carl asked.

"Our department contracts out our DNA testing with a local lab," Burgess said. "My friends there were nice enough to give me a heads up on the influx of paternity tests they've been getting."

"Oh," Carl said. It had not occurred to him how many people might hear about a case like this and decide they must be victims of the same crime. A lot of people just don't get along with their kids, and most of them would love it if they could blame it on anyone else.

"I asked them to slow-walk it for me," Burgess said, "but there's only so much stalling they can do. It's only a matter of time before they have to start returning results."

"You think it's going to be bad?" Carl asked.

"It's already bad," Burgess said. "And I've been doing this long enough to know that for every victim we know about, there's a dozen more we don't know about."

"Who's your lead investigator on this?" Carl asked.

"I took this one myself," Burgess said. "I've got a special place at the bottom of my boot for kidnappers."

"Alright then," Carl said, "I've got some questions."

"Fire away," Burgess said, leaning back in his chair.

"How come there aren't any statements from hospital staff?" Carl asked.

"Well, those stupid lawyers filed the civil lawsuit first," Burgess said. "So all the staff had already been told not to say anything without permission from lawyers, union reps, and priests first."

"They're more worried about losing a lawsuit than the safety of those children," Carl said, frowning.

"They can't help anybody if they get sued out of business," Burgess said.

"Like I said," Carl said, "root of all evil. Second question, how did they know?"

"Who?" Burgess asked.

"The parents," Carl said. "How did they know to do a DNA screening on their newborns?"

"If you find out," Burgess said. "I'd love to know. They get all squirrelly and weird when I ask; saying things like 'gut feeling' and 'a mother's intuition.'"

"You didn't press them on it?" Carl asked.

"You got kids, Abrams?" Burgess asked.

"No," Carl said.

"How about parents?" Burgess asked.

"I have parents, yes," Carl said.

"So, how would you feel," Burgess said, "if one day your parents turned to you and said we think you might not belong in this family?"

"That would be a pretty shitty day," Carl said.

"Exactly," Burgess said. "And any parent who even thinks that feels like shit for thinking it. So, no, I didn't press them on it. Nobody wants to talk about the day they looked at their own child and rejected them. It's a shitty day for everyone."

"I get what you're saying there, Lieutenant," Carl said. "But I think they're more than just embarrassed. I think they're hiding something."

"How do you mean?" Burgess asked.

"I'm looking at the filing from the civil case," Carl said, "and the DNA tests are all within a week of each other."

"What?" Burgess asked.

"If these people all had a hunch or a bad feeling," Carl said, handing the file back to the lieutenant, "they all had it at the same time."

Burgess looked down at the pages that Carl had indicated.

"Holy shit," he said. "Someone tipped them off. Why wouldn't they tell us?"

"That is a damn good question, isn't it?" Carl said. "Whoever it is, they are definitely the first person we should be talking to. How soon can we bring some parents in here for questioning?"

"We should probably go to them," Burgess said. "These are all pretty well-to-do families with real nasty lawyers. They're more likely to talk to us as long as we keep it looking like we're on their side."

"Aren't we on their side?" Carl asked.

"I'm on the side of the missing kids," Burgess said. "I know everyone likes to think that parents will always put their kids first, but I'm not falling for that anymore."

"Glad to see we're on the same page, Lieutenant," Carl said, standing. "I'm going to go check in to my hotel and read up on the rest of the case files. Call me when you've set up an interview."

"Will do, Agent," Burgess said. "Before you go, let me ask you, have you ever been to Landfall before?"

"Twice before," Abrams said, "Last time was about four years ago."

"So then, you know about the tunnels?" Burgess said.

"I know about the tunnels," Carl said, nodding.

The Landfall tunnels were part urban legend, part local politics football, and part municipal screw-up of historic measure. The history and rumors that surrounded the tunnels were as convoluted and labyrinthine as the tunnels themselves, but all ended at the same conclusion; nobody in their right mind would ever set foot in them.

The city had done their best to barricade off all of the entrances to the tunnels, but one of the many, frustrating charms of the city was that nobody could say with any certainty just how many of them there were. Every election cycle, no small part of the political debate would swirl around what the hell to do about the tunnels. But no matter which candidate's agenda was elected, there was always some sort of bureaucratic or budgetary meltdown that prevented anything from being done. And so, the denizens of Landfall simply had to resign themselves to avoiding them, and doing their best to warn visitors away from them.

"Good," Burgess said. "I lost an ATF agent down there for four days last year. I'd appreciate it if you didn't put me through that again."

Carl nodded, and left the building.

* * *

The hotel was only a few blocks from Police HQ, but the dark clouds covering the city were threatening to start pouring down on him. Carl contemplated if he wanted to head directly to the hotel, or chance taking a detour to a Cajun food cart that he'd come to love when he was last in the city. He had forgotten how wet the city tended to be, and hadn't brought an umbrella with him.

But, Leon's shrimp gumbo was the best Carl had ever had outside of New Orleans. It was worth the risk.

"Oh, shit," Leon said as Carl approached the cart. "It's good to see you again, Agent Carl. But if you're back in town, maybe I should go on vacation for a while."

"Don't worry Leon," Carl said. "No big threats this time. I'm looking for missing kids this time."

"Dang," Leon said. "Glad I don't have your job."

As Leon scooped a serving of gumbo into a to-go bowl, Carl scanned over the surrounding blocks. The city certainly had its charm, if you could manage to look at it with "soft eyes" as his grandmother used to say. If you can manage to not focus on the underlying confusion, anger, anxiety, and delirium of the inhabitants, and the subtle aggression of the architecture, the city has its own way of being beautiful. For every sharp angle, there was bud on a tree just waiting to blossom. For every angry, tattoo-covered face, there was a childlike delight behind their eyes. The city was fierce in its cultural rebellion, but it was happy to have found itself. One of Carl's old partners had called it "a city of mismatched socks," and he'd meant it as a compliment.

"You know the missing kids I'm talking about, right?" Carl asked Leon as he packaged up the order.

"I read the papers," Leon said.

"Have you heard anything that wasn't in the papers?"

Carl asked.

"Nah, man," Leon said. "This is Hill People problems."

Another of the Landfall charms was the ironic use of the term "Hill People." Elsewhere in the country, such a term meant uneducated and isolated. In Landfall, it meant people who lived in the most expensive real estate in the city; the hills to the west of downtown.

"You know anybody getting scared, though?" Carl asked. "Panicking and getting their kids tested?"

"Folks under the watermark haven't got the money for a DNA test," Leon said, frowning, "Best just to not think about it."

"I suppose not," Carl said. "One more question; that guy on the other side of the street that's making grumpy faces at me, do you know him?"

Leon made as subtle of a glance up as he could before forcing his gaze back down to Carl. He didn't have to look long, the guy was unmissable. Carl had spotted him as soon as he'd stepped out of the station. He'd assumed at first that he was some random Landfall citizen that hated cops, but he was still there when Carl reached the food cart, that look of utter disdain radiating from his face directly at Carl.

"Oh shit, that guy," Leon said. "I don't know his name, but he's not somebody I'd want to stand too close to."

"He's trouble?" Carl asked.

"I don't know if he's trouble," Leon said, "but I've seen some shit happen when he's around. And that sonofabitch can take a hit, let me tell you."

"What do you mean?" Carl asked.

"About a year ago," Leon said, "I saw him bolt past here with a couple of huge motherfuckers tryin' to run him down. I never heard what went down, but they were super-pissed at him. Pissed enough to follow right behind him when he ran into traffic."

"He ran them into traffic," Carl said, his eyebrow arching up. "On *this* street?"

"All three of them got mowed down," Leon said. "The two big guys, they got carted away in ambulances. But that guy got up and walked away before anybody even knew what happened."

"Holy shit," Carl said.

"Amen," Leon said.

"I don't suppose you could try to overhear his name for me?" Carl asked.

"I could try, but no promises," Leon said. "I don't want him to come headbutt my cart or something."

"I appreciate you either way," Carl said, picking up his package of food.

The rain started to fall just as Carl was crossing to the next block. He took the opportunity to stop and button up his coat, glancing at the reflective surface of the office building next to him to see that The Grumpy Face was keeping close by, staying almost exactly one block behind him, on the other side of the street.

There was nothing particularly descriptive about him. He wasn't a large man, but not particularly small either. His complexion was pale, but no more pale than anyone else living in a perpetually cloud-covered city. He looked to be in his early twenties, but moved like someone much older. Where Carl had developed a skill at looking non-assuming, this guy seemed to have a natural talent for it.

Hair-colored hair, Carl thought to himself. He might never have noticed him, were it not for the perpetual scowl that seemed to be blaming Carl for the breakup of his favorite band.

After adjusting his coat to shield him from the rain, Carl continued on to the hotel, taking the chance to glance at every shop window he passed to see that The Local was still keeping pace behind him.

Less than a block from the hotel, Carl's phone rang.

"Got the trace back on the number you gave me," Burgess said.

"Did I win anything?" Carl asked.

"The number is assigned to a VoIP company based out of Italy," Burgess said. "We'd have to invoke the NATO treaty to get any more than that."

"Well, that's to be expected, I guess," Carl said. "That's actually the least weird part of this, so far."

"You said the cabby gave you the number?" Burgess asked. "The cabby that you picked at random as you left the airport."

"That's right," Carl said, "Who said that someone gave it to him yesterday. I got this assignment this morning, so whoever it was knew I was coming before I did."

"Curiouser and curiouser," Burgess quoted.

"Welcome to Landfall, right?" Carl said.

"That sounds derogatory when you say it, Abrams," Burgess said.

"Hey," Carl continued, "do you know about a case from about a year ago where three guys run into traffic on Second Street, but one of them walks away from it."

"Oh yeah, The Sokolov brothers," Burgess said. "Real piece of work, those two. We'd been watching them for illegal gambling for years, but never managed to get our hands on anything solid. Them getting stuck in the hospital for three weeks gave us the chance we needed. Last I heard they were both still in wheelchairs in the hospital wing of the State Pen."

"Did you ever find the third guy?" Carl asked.

"No idea who it was," Burgess said. "The Sokolov's even said they didn't know his name, just that he was a bastard and they wouldn't rest until blah blah blah, you know. Couldn't even get a solid description of the guy. All anybody would say is that he was 'a normal looking dude.'"

"How many 'normal looking' people are there in Landfall, Lieutenant?" Carl asked.

"It really sounds bad when you say it like that," Burgess said, "Where'd you hear about this, anyway?"

"Making conversation with the locals," Carl said. "I just got to my hotel. I'll see you tomorrow."

Carl hung up the phone and chanced an obvious look around the street. The Grumpy Face was nowhere to be seen. It was probably just as well. If this guy was as tough as Leon made him sound, it was probably a bad idea to confront him without backup. Carl felt confident he'd get another chance in the future.

The lobby of The Stanton Hotel looked like a fancy bourbon commercial; polished wood paneling and fancy lampshades in all directions. The bar was just to one side of the lobby, and was playing host to a dozen or so business-class-types who were already drinking like their tax-deductible expense accounts depended on it. The noise was notable, but not quite raucous yet.

"Checking in?" the front desk agent perked up at the sight of Carl. His name tag read "ISAAC" in all capital letters, like it was yelling.

"Carl Abrams," Carl said. "I should have a government account."

"Carl Abrams, FBI," the clerk announced with dramatic pride, clicking away at the monitor in front of him. "It looks like your luggage arrived earlier, and we've taken the liberty of putting it in your room."

"Yeah, sure," Carl said, "is there anywhere more quiet I can get a drink? I've got some files I need to look over."

"Big case, huh?" Isaac said, excitedly. "Gotta hunt down that one crucial clue that the local beat cops missed, right?"

"I'm not at liberty to say," Carl said. He had neither the time nor the energy to deal with this right now.

"Ah, a by-the-book G-Man," Isaac said. "I like that. Our restaurant is on the second floor. It usually stays pretty quiet, and they can get anything you want from the bar."

"Perfect," Carl said.

Isaac placed a key card into a small envelope and wrote Carl's room number on it.

"Can I ask you a question?" Isaac said, placing the envelope on the desk in front of Carl.

"It's a free country," Carl said, already afraid that this may never end.

"Those ads they put at the beginning of DVDs," Isaac said, quietly. "Do you guys really bust down doors for copying movies?"

Carl sighed. "Depends how many movies you copied," he said. "If you keep it under ten, we'll knock before we arrest you."

"Thanks for the tip," Isaac said, looking far too excited by the answer. "Enjoy your stay, and good luck catching the bad guys."

Carl picked up the envelope and made his way to the elevators.

"Welcome to Landfall," he muttered to himself.

CHAPTER TWO
FAMILY SECRETS

The home of Ray and Donna Swain had a view of the city that was worth a million dollars all on its own. But Carl couldn't help but fixate on the fact that the house was on stilts, on the side of a hill that looked like it would melt like ice cream if it rained too much. And it hadn't stopped raining since Carl had gotten to town. He couldn't imagine why anyone would pay any money for that kind of stress, let alone a million dollars.

"This is Special Agent Carl Abrams," Burgess said, introducing Carl to the couple. "The FBI is aiding in this case, so he's just here to do a follow-up."

"Where's the kid?" Carl asked. He already knew the answer to the question, but he wanted to see for himself how the parents reacted to the mention of the replacement baby.

"What?" Donna Swain asked, looking genuinely hurt and confused by the question.

"The fake baby," Carl said. "The one your son was replaced with. Where is he?"

"Jesus, Abrams," Burgess murmured. Carl had planned to

phrase the question much more diplomatically, but the combination of the hypnotic view of the city and the paralyzing fear of being trapped inside a house that was crumbling down the hillside had made him stupid.

"Child services took him," Ray Swain said. "We offered to adopt him. There's plenty of room here, but they said we couldn't."

"Technically, he's a kidnap victim too," Burgess said to Carl. "Until we find out who his real parents are, he's a ward of the state."

"If we'd have known," Donna said, almost swallowing her words. "We might not've-- We didn't think we'd lose both of our sons."

The hurt in Donna Swain's voice snapped Carl out of it. He tore his gaze away from the wall of windows and forced himself not to think about any of the people living downhill from this deathtrap.

"I'm sorry," Carl said. "That was very insensitive of me. If you'd like to do this another time..."

"No," Ray said. "Let's get this over with. I want you out there finding our son. We'll worry about...the other one...once this is all settled."

Carl nodded and opened the file folder. Inside were the detailed accounts the Swain's had already given to their lawyers and to the PD earlier. There were handwritten notations in the margins where the stories didn't quite match, or changed between interviews, but nothing significant that couldn't easily be the failure of common memory.

The story was pretty straight-forward; the baby was born and immediately put through the usual hell that all babies are put through at the moment of birth. A vinyl syringe was stuck up his nose to suck the goo out, disinfectant paste was smeared into his eyes, a needle pricked into his foot for a blood sample, and a thermometer was shoved up his ass for good measure. Welcome to life, little guy.

All that was done right in the birthing suite in under two minutes, ending with a plastic ring marked "Harrison Swain" locked around his ankle and a blanket swaddled around him before being placed in his exhausted mother's arms for the first time. If that was the moment he'd been swapped out for another baby, it would've taken a conspiracy between the entire hospital staff and a Vegas magician to pull it off.

From there, the entire family was taken together from the birthing suite to a hospital room, where the baby and mother seemingly never left each other's side for the two nights that their insurance allowed them to stay. The first night, Ray slept on a couch in the hospital room, and on the second he went home to prepare the house for the whole family.

That would have been the most likely time for the babies to have been switched; when mother and child were left alone, with mother still hooked up to an IV to manage any lingering pain or anxiety. But, by that time, Donna had spent two whole days with her newborn, and swears that she would notice if her baby looked any different that following morning. She would bet her life that the baby they took home that day was the baby that was put in her arms one minute after it was born.

And yet, the baby that had the name "Harrison Swain" around his ankle when they brought him home was not Harrison Swain.

"Have you ever been on any kind of narcotics before, Mrs. Swain?" Carl asked.

"What do you mean?" Donna asked, confused.

"I mean, recreationally," Carl clarified.

"Well, I mean," Donna said, "I've tried a few things here and there. When I was a teenager, but nothing that serious, if that's what you mean."

"So," Carl continued, "if you were on something that inhibited your senses, or incapacitated you in any way, you wouldn't know how to recognize it."

"No, I don't suppose I would," Donna said, clearly uncomfortable with what Carl was suggesting.

"Mr. Swain," Carl said, turning to Ray. "Did your wife seem at all out of character while you were at the hospital?"

"In what way?" Ray asked.

"Was she..." Carl tried to think of how to phrase it, "stupid?"

"Excuse me?" Donna blurted.

"Abrams," Burgess growled.

"Giddy!" Carl suddenly said. "I meant giddy. I should have said 'giddy' just then. Was she over-the-top happy and personable? Did she seem like she was high?"

"We'd just had a baby," Ray said. "We'd been planning for this for three years. It was the best day of our lives."

"It's also exhausting," Carl said, "and sometimes a little traumatizing. Most women, after giving birth, can barely stay awake."

Neither of them said anything. They just looked at each other. Carl could see that they were both afraid to say what they were thinking. They didn't want to upset each other. Carl didn't need to press it any further. Without going back in time to get a blood test, there was no way to confirm it anyway.

"After you got home from the hospital," Carl moved on, "did you experience any postpartum depression?"

"What does that have to do with anything?" Ray asked.

Carl could see now that he was starting to strain on the good will that Burgess told him to preserve.

"I'm sorry," Carl said. "It's important, I promise."

"We already told you," Ray growled. "It was the happiest day of our lives."

"I'm sure it was," Carl said. "But what about the next day? Or the week after? Once you were settled at home, how did you feel then?"

"I was fine," Donna said.

"You're sure?" Carl said. "It's nothing to be ashamed of. Half of new mothers experience this, it's very common."

"She said she was fine," Ray barked.

Carl sighed. He tried. He had genuinely tried to give them every benefit of the doubt.

"Then what the hell did you get a DNA test for?" he asked.

The Swains fell silent in shock.

"I mean, postpartum makes sense," Carl continued. "You start to feel like you don't have a bond with your baby. You get paranoid. That happens. You'd be surprised how often that happens. But if you're telling me that didn't happen to you, then why did you get a DNA test? The filing from your lawyer just says you 'became suspicious.' What made you suspicious? What made you and seven other families suspicious all at the same time?"

They didn't say anything. They weren't even looking at each other anymore. They were looking at the floor. Whatever it was they were hiding, they were too ashamed to even admit it to each other.

"We don't have much to go on here," Carl said. "If someone told you that you had the wrong baby, we need to know who they are."

"We never met them," Donna whispered. "They sent us a letter."

"They sent a what now?" Carl said.

"We got a letter in the mail," Ray confirmed. "It told us he wasn't our baby."

"A letter?" Carl said. "Like, with a stamp?"

The Swains nodded.

"Who was the letter from?" Burgess asked, finally trying to be helpful.

"We don't know," Ray said. "It was postmarked in town, but there was no return address."

"Why didn't you mention this before?" Burgess pressed.

They didn't answer. Again, they just looked shamefully at the ground.

"Well," Carl said. "We're going to need to get that letter."

Ray gulped and seemed to need to steel himself before he answered.

"I'll have my lawyer send you the relevant parts," he said, calmly.

"Your lawyer?" Burgess said.

"The relevant parts?" Carl asked. "If this letter is real, then the whole damn thing is the most important evidence we've got."

"There was other material in the letter that is private," Ray said.

"Excuse me?" Carl said. "What does that even mean?"

"They knew things," Donna said, her voice just barely above a whisper. "Things that nobody could have known."

"What kind of things?" Burgess asked.

"Personal things," Donna said, sounding more impatient than ashamed.

"What could possibly be in that letter," Carl asked, "that's more important than your son?"

"My lawyer will contact you," Ray said. "Please leave my home now."

"You better hope that this doesn't--" Carl started.

"That's enough, Abrams," Burgess stopped him. "Let's go."

Carl fumed as he collected up the file and marched out of the stupid house with Burgess.

"Okay, so," Carl said once they were in Burgess' car, "That was weird, right? And I don't mean Landfall weird, I mean actually fucking weird."

"It was pretty fucking weird," Burgess agreed. "Do you think your mysterious phone number guy has something to do with this?"

"Would it be weirder if he is?" Carl said, throwing his hands up. "I'm honestly asking here, because I really don't know."

"It's gotta be someone on hospital staff," Burgess said. "You can learn a lot about someone from their medical records."

"Maybe," Carl said. "A whistleblower would almost make sense, but this is a fucked up way to go about it. How long until we can start questioning hospital staff?"

"Lawyers are still fighting it out," Burgess said. "The hospital wants to script the questions and have all the transcripts under seal."

Carl nodded. "So we can't hand over any findings to the civil case," he said. "Yeah, I've seen that bullshit before."

"All eight of them," Burgess said. "All eight families didn't say a word about a letter. Were the Swain's the only ones who got a letter, or are they all that freaked out by them."

"We've got seven more chances to find out," Carl said, pulling out the stack of files from his briefcase. "Did any of them seem especially timid? Like they'd likely break under pressure?"

"These are Hill People," Burgess said. "Even the timid looking ones will have your badge for not complimenting their drapes. Hell, the Swains get their butts personally kissed by the Mayor. That's why we came to see them first; so they'll tell him how I'm personally seeing to this case for them. Thank you, by the way, for fucking that up for me."

"For what it's worth," Carl said. "I'll miss you when you're gone."

* * *

Another great view. More dumb stilts. Carl wondered if Hill People got a thrill out of cheating death every minute of every day.

The Conrads were the fifth family on the list. It became quickly apparent that the Swains had already spread the word about what had happened. One family after another refused to let them in the door, only saying that their lawyer would contact them with the "relevant" information. They, of course, all meant the same lawyer.

James Conrad was the first to not seem terrified at the idea of talking about "The Letter." He was alone when Carl and Burgess arrived. His scandalously younger wife was at her yoga class, so he invited them in to talk in private.

"You have to understand the position we're in," James Conrad said. He walked slowly across the room and settled into a chair that seemed almost as old as he was. It was the only thing Carl could see in the house that wasn't brand new.

"I'm not too keen on offending my fellow litigants."

"Why is everyone so afraid that these letters get out?" Carl asked. "What's in them?"

"I don't know what's in the others," James said, "but our lawyer seemed to think that if they were included in the lawsuit, the hospital could use them to discredit all of us."

"What was in yours?" Burgess asked.

"You mean, besides telling us our daughter wasn't our daughter?" James smirked. "Nothing too colorful. Just a few details about how my wife and I met that she'd prefer not be gossiped about."

"How would someone find out about these details?" Carl asked.

"I'm sure I have no idea," James said. "It seems like nobody really can have any secrets these days."

"Did you mention any of it to any hospital staff?" Burgess asked.

"Not that I can think of," James said. "My wife can be a bit of a talker, though. A real people-person, that one."

"But she's the one who wants to keep it a secret," Carl said.

"Usually," James nodded.

"If you don't mind me asking," Carl said, "what is the detail in question?"

James sighed. "Kayla was my student when we met," he said. "Nothing happened between us until after she graduated, but still. There it is. We tell people that we met for the first time at her younger sister's graduation. That is when we first started...you know. But, even as salacious as that is on its own, it makes life a little easier to leave out the finer details."

"Did the author of the letter threaten to let that

information out somehow?" Burgess asked.

"Not at all," James said. "They just wanted to make sure we took them seriously. In fact, I got the impression that they were quite apologetic about it all."

"What did they say to give you that impression?" Carl asked.

"Nothing specific," James said, waving his hand dismissively. "I teach Language and Letters at the University. Deconstructing a writer's motivation is kinda my thing."

"I don't suppose you'll let us see the letter," Burgess asked.

James sighed again. "I really wish I could," he said. "Kayla's been spending ten hours a day at yoga since Child Services came and took the baby away. I'd very much like to see this resolved, and get my family back together. But I'm worried that the other parents will shut us out if we don't follow their lead."

"What if you took the lead?" Carl asked. "Do you think you can talk some sense into them?"

"I suppose I could try," James said. "I don't know what else to do with myself."

"Thank you, Mr. Conrad," Burgess said. "You've been a big help."

"Godspeed, gentlemen," James said, looking more tired than anything else.

Carl wondered if a mudslide would be doing him a favor.

* * *

"Anyone with social network savvy could've gotten that," Carl said, as they drove away.

"I already knew it," Burgess said.

"Really?" Carl asked.

"I did background on all the parents," Burgess said. "I was trying to find a connection, like maybe they all went to the same country club or something. By the way, they all go to the same country club. They all frequent the same high-end restaurants, the same golf club, and the same movie theater. I don't think any of them have been below the watermark in their lives."

Carl nodded. Landfall tried its hardest to look like a big city, but in truth it was a small town. Plenty of great sushi bars, but they all got their fish off the same boat. That was part of its charm, alongside the manic-depressive cast of characters that lived there. It was Disneyland for David Foster Wallace fans.

"So," Carl said, "we've got a possible inside man that tries to warn a bunch of parents that they took home babies that weren't theirs, but first they do background research on all of them to make sure they're good and paranoid when they get the news."

"It's a really screwed up way of doing things," Burgess said. "I mean, if they knew the kids got swapped, why not tell them where their real kids are? Why give us eight missing kids and eight orphans."

"Did eight more parents get letters that we don't know about yet?" Carl asked out loud.

"This doesn't feel like a shuffle game," Burgess said. "My gut tells me these kids were full-on stolen, and the other kids were left as decoys."

"But why?" Carl said. "I mean, if we're talking about some Black Market baby adoption scam, why not just sell the babies you already have? What's with the 'take a baby, leave a baby' operation?"

"We need to find who wrote those letters," Burgess said. "I feel like I might lose my mind with this one."

"We need to question the hospital staff," Carl said. "It doesn't make any sense unless it's one of them. We just need to give the whistleblower a chance to speak up on the record."

Burgess was quiet for a moment.

"You should call the number," he finally said.

"I'm not calling the number," Carl responded. "I don't have time for a Cloak And Dagger pissing contest. Especially since I don't actually know if this even has anything to do with that."

"Like you said before," Burgess said. "It might be weirder if it didn't."

"I've dealt with anonymous tip shit before," Carl said. "I'm not a fan. We'll question the staff, and they can come forward then. We'll get this on the record, through proper procedure. I'm not going to have some crackhead defense attorney tear my case apart over improper channels."

"If you say so," Burgess said. "I'll let the DA know we're desperate. Maybe they can give in to one or two of the hospital's demands if it means we get one-on-one time with our insider."

"No script," Carl said. "I ask the questions I want to ask. They can have their sealed records, I don't give a shit about the civil case anymore."

"I'll tell them you said that," Burgess nodded.

They rode in silence for a moment, weaving through traffic back to HQ.

"How are the kids doing?" Carl asked, suddenly. "The orphans. Are they going to be okay?"

"My wife works in Child Services," Burgess said. "They're

in good hands."

"Good," Carl said. "One less thing to worry about."

CHAPTER THREE
NIGHT SHIFT NURSES

Carl's hands felt stiff as he dialed the phone. He had been clenching them for hours without even realizing it.

Once they'd gotten out of sight of the hospital, Carl had made Burgess pull over to the nearest parking lot. They'd ended up at a convenience store with a name that suggested it wasn't affiliated with any franchise. Carl paced the parking lot, shaking his hands out as he waited for his supervisor to answer the phone.

"It's gone to voicemail," Carl said, hanging up the phone.

"Does the FBI not leave messages?" Burgess said, leaning casually against his car.

"I need to talk to someone about this now," Carl said.

They'd had to wait for two days before they got their interviews with the hospital staff. Carl had passed the time reading up on Burgess' background research on the victims' families and arguing with their lawyer about access to the mysterious letters. When he got really bored, he would go out for strolls around the city to catch sight of Mr. Grumpy

Face, and make as much of a show as possible at ignoring him.

Over the course of ten hours, Carl and Burgess visited all three hospitals. They interviewed a dozen maternity staff members at each hospital, with lawyers and union representatives watching over them, and learned absolutely nothing new from any of them. The hospital was an airtight operation, and there was no possible way any baby could ever be kidnapped from their facility, except for the eight times they were.

"Isn't it, like, midnight over there?" Burgess asked. The interviews needed to include both daytime and nighttime staff, so they'd been scheduled for as much overlap between the shifts that they could manage. This meant starting in the late afternoon and going well past dinnertime.

"It's only eleven," Carl replied. He dialed his supervisor's number again, attempting to force his willpower through the phone to make it ring louder.

"This is Thompson," a voice finally answered.

"It's Abrams," Carl said. "I have a situation."

"Is it a matter of National Security?" Thompson asked.

Carl wanted to say yes. He very nearly said yes.

"No, not quite," Carl said.

"Then why are you calling me after hours?" Thompson said.

"Look, Director," Carl said, only realizing just now that he'd made the call without even thinking about what he was going to say. "I think this case might be a bigger deal than we'd first assessed."

"You're working on those missing infants in Landfall, right?" Thompson said.

"Yes, sir," Carl said, "and I have reason to believe that a

local White Supremacy group may be involved."

Thompson didn't respond right away. He was quiet for the span of three heartbeats before taking a very thoughtful breath.

"Your first case off the Domestic Terrorism Task Force," Thompson said, "and you just happen to stumble upon a domestic terrorist group."

"The odds aren't that low, sir," Carl said. "There was a reason we had the task force to begin with."

"You understand why I'm skeptical though, right?" Thompson said.

"I absolutely understand, sir," Carl said. "But, I've got a bad feeling here."

"Have you ever come across White Power groups involved in mass kidnapping?" Thompson asked.

"Many times," Carl said. "A lot of them fund their operations through sex trafficking."

"I'm aware of that," Thompson said. "But these aren't immigrant teenagers. These are white babies from well-to-do white families. When have you ever seen White Fundamentalists kidnapping white babies?"

Carl racked his brain for any case that would fall under that association, but he had to admit defeat there.

"None," Carl said. "But it's not like they haven't evolved before. I promise I'm not just grasping at straws here. Fifteen years of experience is telling me this is the real thing. I really think you should get the task force involved in this right away."

Thompson sighed. "I need more than just your gut feeling," he said. "Especially at this time of night. Tell me what you have so far."

Carl dug his notebook out of his jacket pocket and laid it

out on the hood of Burgess' car. Flipping through the pages, he found the beginning of his interview notes.

"There were three hospitals involved," Carl began. "Two kids taken from one, three each from the other two. We were allowed to question key staff members of the first, second, and third shift of each maternity ward with legal council and union representation present."

"For Christ's sake, Abrams," Thompson interrupted. "I'm in my pajamas, just get to the point."

"Okay," Carl said, taking a breath to steady himself. "It was the night shift staff. They had to come in during the day, before their shifts, for the interviews."

"Go on," Thompson said.

"One of them, I'm not kidding, came in wearing a tank top," Carl said. "Not even a regular tank top, I mean an undershirt. He came in practically in his underwear."

"If he was a night-shift worker," Thompson said, "From his perspective you were interviewing him in the middle of the night. Did you really expect him to dress up for it?"

"It's not just that," Carl said. "The guy came into his interview with his tattoos showing."

Thompson took a moment to take that in. "He had some White Power tats, I take it?" he asked.

"An obscure one," Carl said. "He had a Wolfsangel insignia on his tricep."

"Wolfsangel?" Thompson asked.

"It was a heraldic symbol used by an early incarnation of the SS," Carl said. "Basically, pro-Nazi street thugs that would bust up protests and intimidate dissenters before Hitler took full power."

"If it's a lesser-known symbol all by itself, how can you be sure?" Thompson asked. "My kid almost got a Russian

Mob tattoo because he thought it looked cool."

"There's more," Carl said. "After spotting the first one, I...checked the rest of the staff."

"Excuse me?" Thompson said. "You strip searched the hospital staff?"

"Not to that extent, no," Carl said. "I just, sort of, told their union reps that I wanted to check for needle marks. I wanted to make sure there were no addicts on staff. Because addicts might be enticed to steal babies for drug money."

"You're killing me here, Abrams," Thompson said.

"Director," Carl said, "I found the same tattoo on at least one night shift staff member at all three hospitals. One of the hospitals had two. Two nurses. Not orderlies, not janitors; nurses. And those are just the ones I was able to see on their arms and shoulders."

"That's still pretty thin, Agent," Thompson said. "There's no law against tattoos."

"Director, it can't be a coincidence," Carl said. "All three hospitals have skinheads on the night staff?"

Thompson heaved a sigh into the phone. He was losing interest in the conversation, or patience, or both.

"I'm trying to help you here, Carl," Thompson said. Carl could not remember the last time the director had called him by his first name. "You're not on the task force anymore. If you're seriously telling me that this is a Supremacist operation, then that means you're off the case."

That had not occurred to Carl. He had assumed he would simply be augmented unofficially back into the Task Force for this case. That sort of thing happened all the time. Investigations constantly evolve and develop as new information comes to light. Inter-departmental cooperation wasn't just routine, it was practically a daily occurrence.

"But this is my case," Carl said. "I've got the experience and the local connections. Why wouldn't I just--"

"You're off the task force, Agent," Thompson said. "You don't get to sneak back in on a technicality. If this really is a White Power Conspiracy, then you're to head back to D.C. on the next flight."

It was the first time that it had ever occurred to Carl that his removal from the Task Force might have been more than just politics or "budget cuts." Maybe it was personal. Maybe there really was someone who had a grudge against him. It's not like the FBI is completely free of people who might casually mention that "Hitler wasn't *all* bad," but as far as he knew, Carl had never made any genuine enemies there.

"Wouldn't I at least stick around long enough to get the Task Force up to speed?" Carl asked.

"There's no telling when that will be," Thompson said. "The Task Force doesn't have the resources to chase down every wacky scheme these nutjobs get up to."

"Director, you can't be serious," Carl said. "You're seriously telling me to just walk away from this? They are kidnapping infants for God-knows-what here."

"I'm sure the local authorities can handle it," Thompson said. "You were only there at their request to begin with. This is their case, not yours."

Carl glanced over at Burgess, who was making a show of watching the foot traffic that passed them by, and certainly not listening in on Carl's phone call.

"I'll ask you again, Agent," Thompson said. "Are you *sure* this case involves a White Power group?"

"I could be mistaken," Carl heard himself say.

"That's what I thought," Thompson said. "Stay in your lane, Abrams. Am I clear?"

"Yes, sir," Carl said.

"Good," Thompson said, and the call abruptly ended.

"Did you get grounded?" Burgess asked as Carl dropped his phone on the hood of the car in frustration.

"I'm not crazy, am I?" Carl asked. "You saw them too. That many in a row can't be a coincidence, right?"

"It's weird, I'll grant you that," Burgess said. "But this state has had a White Power problem for a long time. Don't get me wrong, Landfall is a great place, but it's got its fair share of assholes."

"It's just..." Carl was already tired of sounding like a broken record. "Maybe if it was just one hospital. Even two I could write off as a coincidence. But all three? All three night shifts are sporting Nazi tats?"

"Look," Burgess said. "We shouldn't be yakkin' about a case out in the open like this. I know a place not too far from here that's cop-friendly. Let's go get a drink."

Carl looked around them for the first time since they got out of the car. They were in a mostly residential neighborhood, and people were glancing over at them with interest as they walked by with their dogs. A pair of teenage girls sitting on a bus bench stared right at them, transfixed by Carl's near-meltdown.

"If I start drinking now," Carl said. "I'm afraid I might not stop."

"That's pretty much the point," Burgess said, already climbing into the driver's seat.

* * *

The Angry Onion was everything Carl expected a neighborhood bar in Landfall to be. Not the usual tourist trappings or high-dollar destination luxuries of a downtown tavern or club. This was a place for pure blood Landfall residents to have a quiet drink after a long day.

It wasn't a very big bar. Maybe a half-dozen tables were pushed to one side, with most of the floor space being taken up by two pool tables and a small stage with a stripper pole. The bar itself took up the entire longest wall to the left of the entrance, and was just barely lit enough to display the many, many bottles that were arranged against the obligatory mirror-backed shelves. Some sort of heavy metal music was playing from the speakers behind the stage, but they were turned down so patrons didn't have to shout when they talked.

"Grab us a table," Burgess said, as they entered. "I'll get the first round."

It was well past Happy Hour by the time Carl and Burgess walked in. There was one elderly man wearing overalls at the bar, who seemed only interested in staring at his own reflection behind the bar as he occasionally sipped from the bottle of domestic beer in front of him. A middle-aged couple was casually playing pool at one of the tables, and the one stripper on duty that night sat lackadaisically on the edge of the stage, watching them as they played. The bartender was the flashiest person in the entire bar. A gray-haired ponytail sprouted from the top of her head and fell all the way to the middle of her back, and the studded leather jacket she wore was out-sparkled by the sequined halter-top peering out from under it. She looked like she might have been a stripper herself, in her youth. Though, Carl estimated that to have been approximately two-hundred years ago.

Carl took a seat at one of the tables near the wall. This wasn't the sort of place that made him feel paranoid, but taking a seat where you can observe all of the other patrons, as well as the exits, was just a matter of habit for him now.

Carl risked a glance over to the stripper that was not stripping. Being the professional that she is, immediately caught his glance and winked at him. He gave her a friendly nod back and turned his attention away just in time to see Burgess approaching with two pints of beer.

"I would've gotten us some fries," Burgess said, setting the drinks on the table and taking a seat, "but they got the worst food in town. They can't even do fries right."

"Why do you come here, then?" Carl asked.

"It's cop friendly," Burgess said. "Nobody likes cops in Landfall. This town is..."

Burgess trailed off, seeming to think twice about what he was about to say. He glanced around the room and offered his own obligatory nod to the stripper before leaning in towards Carl.

"Real talk," Burgess said. "We're not in the office. We're not on the clock. This is just you and me, two professionals, having a drink. Right?"

"The record is officially off," Carl nodded.

Burgess nodded and took a drink of his beer. "I came to Landfall twenty years ago," he said. "And just like everybody else, I was blown away at what a kooky place it was. Hell, my first day on the job, I walk out of the station and almost get run over by a dude on a unicycle. A fucking unicycle."

"I've seen them around," Carl said.

"Don't get me wrong," Burgess said. "I've come to love the place. I can't imagine living anywhere else. I mean, look." He waved his hand toward the stripper, still not bothering to dance for the non-existent audience. "You can't get this anywhere else. A friendly neighborhood bar that also has a stripper."

"Yeah," Carl said. "I keep meaning to ask about that."

"It's a thing they do around here," Burgess said, waving his hand in dismissal. "Now, I've got a theory."

"Go on," Carl said.

"The thing is," Burgess said. "This place ain't that weird."

"Is it legal for you to say that?" Carl asked.

"We're just small," he said. "Los Angeles has weird shit. New York has weird shit. I ain't ever left the country, but I'd bet Paris has got some weird shit. But Landfall is a tenth of the size of most major cities. Every city has punk weirdos, and hippy weirdos, and all kinds of weirdos, but we've got them all in one place. They're not separated by boroughs or districts, they all live in the same fucking building. We have a Chinatown, just like any other city. But ours is only two blocks wide. Two blocks, Abrams. We put giant stone lions out on the sidewalk and call it Chinatown, but it's really just a couple of Chinese takeout places and an Asian-themed strip club."

"Sounds kinda racist," Carl said.

"It's okay, an actual Chinese guy owns it," Burgess said. "But do you get my point? Landfall is no weirder than any other big city that has a thousand different cultures crammed into it. We just have way less space to cram them into, so the place comes off like some kind of circus. And after a few decades of that, well, that's when you start getting a reputation. And when you get a reputation like that, folks got two choices. You either try to gentrify the place, make it all into one small city culture like most other small cities do, or you lean into it. You embrace it. You intentionally try to live up to it. I'm not shitting you, there are folks in this town who wake up in the morning and think, 'what can I do to really weird this place up today?'"

"So it's all an act?" Carl asked.

"Not an act," Burgess said. "More like a game. They're all competing in the Weird Olympics. Gold medal goes to whoever can get the most people to say 'hey, that's weird.'"

"What's that got to do with cops?" Carl asked.

"We're the guys who break up the party," Burgess said. "They're trying to embrace the chaos, and we keep trying to keep it all in order. We wear uniforms, we enforce the law, we tell them they can't block traffic or hang from buildings or live in trees. They see us as the antithesis of what they think this city should represent. Even the folks who've never broken a law in their lives see us as the bad guys. We walk into a bar for a quiet drink, and the place clears out, 'cause nobody wants to drink with us. Eventually, the managers ask us, politely, to stop coming in. Except for this place. This place lets us drink in peace, crappy food and all."

"That's a hell of a sales pitch for one beer," Carl said.

"Yeah," Burgess said. "I think I've been waiting to say that to somebody for a long time. I love this city, I really do. But the city doesn't seem to like me much. After a while, that can start to get to you."

"I know how you feel," Carl said.

"I imagine you do," Burgess said. "So, about these Nazi Nurses."

"Is that what this was really leading up to?" Carl asked. "Let it go Jake, this is Tiny Chinatown?"

"Yes and no," Burgess said. "I'm saying that we've got all kinds here. We seem weird because all kinds are concentrated together. And, unfortunately, 'all kinds' includes racist fuckheads. We don't have any more of them here than any other city, it just seems like we do because we're stuck in a smaller room with them. I don't think it's really that far-fetched to see a bunch of them working in one place. And it probably makes sense to stick them all in the night shift where they're going to piss off the least amount of people."

"You don't think it's weird that the hospital hired that many Neo-Nazis?" Carl asked.

"The hospital might not've known," Burgess said. "We only saw those tats because we went looking for them. As long as their uniforms covered them, and they never said The N-Word on the job, the hospital can't do anything about them. Non-discrimination protections apply to them too."

"Ironically," Carl said.

"Tell me about it," Burgess agreed. "I'll tell you what I do find weird, though."

"I'm listening," Carl said.

"They only had the one," Burgess said. "Never in my life have I seen a skinhead with only one tattoo. What did you call it?"

"The Wolfsangel," Carl said.

"Wolfsangel," Burgess repeated. "Not even a very interesting one, if you ask me. What's it mean?"

"Before Hitler took full power," Carl said, "there was a gang of meatheads he'd use to intimidate anyone who disagreed with him. They'd do a lot of minor damage; vandalism and bar fight type stuff. But mostly they would join in with anti-nazi protests and start a riot in order to give the pro-nazi cops an excuse to arrest everyone. They never publicly displayed themselves as Nazi supporters. They were supposed to blend in with the regular folk and then erupt into chaos when it would do the most damage. They called themselves Werewolves."

"Real original," Burgess burped.

"Well, to be fair," Carl said, "it was the 1930's."

"Did you just say 'to be fair' about the Nazis?" Burgess asked.

"I didn't realize it until it was too late," Carl said.

"So," Burgess said, looking away like he was collecting his thoughts, "it's a symbol that stands for low-key Nazi infiltration. And we just found it on a bunch of maternity ward hospital staff."

"That is precisely what I am losing my shit about," Carl said.

"The problem is," Burgess said, "we have no way of knowing if this infiltration of Nazi Nurses actually has anything at all to do with our missing kids. And your bosses have just told you, in no uncertain terms, to not even consider it as a lead."

"White Supremacists don't kidnap kids from white families," Carl said. "At least, that we've ever seen before."

Burgess sat in silence for a moment as he contemplated all of this.

"I think," Burgess finally said, "I'm going to need a lot more to drink."

CHAPTER FOUR
FRIENDS IN STRANGE PLACES

C arl let Burgess drop him off in front of the hotel. The rain had started up again, and this time Carl was in no mood to walk through it from the station. He'd have to settle for room service food this one time.

"Hey, welcome back," an annoyingly cheery voice said from the desk as Carl entered the lobby. He looked up to see the clerk that had checked Carl in when he first arrived, the name tag still shouting "ISAAC" at the top of its alphabetic lungs.

"You catch those bad guys, G-man?" Isaac said.

"Not at liberty," Carl mumbled, and tried to make his way to the elevators as fast as he could without looking like he was running.

"Oh, wait," Isaac called. "Mr. Abrams. Agent, I mean. We got a package for you."

Carl stopped and sighed. He had almost gotten away.

He turned back just as the clerk produced a small package from behind the front desk. It was a large envelope; the kind with the lining of bubble-wrap inside for mailing electronics.

"Who's it from?" Carl asked as he took the package from Isaac.

"I would never read a guest's mail, sir," Isaac said. "That's a felony."

The package looked innocuous enough. There was no shipping label or return address. Just a postmark to show that it had been mailed in the city, and his name with the address of the hotel handwritten on the front in sharp, jutting letters like an angry child. It may as well have "suspicious package" stamped in big red letters on it.

Carl pulled out his phone and dialed Burgess.

"Miss me already?" Burgess answered.

"Did you mail something to me?" Carl asked.

"Why would I mail you something?" Burgess said. "You work in my office."

"I just got a package at the hotel," Carl said. "Postmarked in town."

"Oh, shit," Burgess said. "Want the bomb squad?"

"It's too small to be a bomb," Carl said. "But it's bigger than your usual Anthrax-type letters. I might just be paranoid."

"Considering who you might have pissed off last time you were in town," Burgess said, "paranoid might be reasonable for you. Want me to come back with a team?"

"No, I've got it covered," Carl said. "If you don't hear back from me, it's either nothing or I'm dead."

"For what it's worth," Burgess said, "I'll miss you when you're gone."

Carl hung up the phone and turned back to Isaac.

"Isaac, can you do a favor for me?" Carl asked.

"That is literally my job, sir," Isaac said, proudly.

"I'd like you to call my room in ten minutes," Carl said.

"If I don't answer, call 911."

Isaac blinked. "Is everything okay?" he asked.

"We'll know in ten minutes," Carl said, and headed to the elevators, trying not to shake the package as he walked.

It took him just under three minutes to ride the elevator to his floor, and make his way down the hall to his room. Inside his room, Carl removed his coat and found a pair of rubber gloves from his forensic kit.

He pulled the bag from the small garbage can by the bed, dumped the garbage out into the can, and laid the plastic bag flat onto the bed. Placing the package onto the plastic, Carl carefully squeezed around the edges of the envelope. He couldn't feel anything that felt like wires, or even any grainy powder sensations. The item in the envelope was small, solid, oblong-ish and alone.

Carl pulled on the gloves and opened his pocket knife. Slitting an opening in the envelope and carefully lifting up the opening, he peered inside.

It was a cell phone. A small, old cell phone.

Carl pulled the phone out of the envelope and examined it. It was a cheap flip-phone, an even older style than what they sold as burner phones these days. It looked like it had seen better days. It was covered in scuffs and scratches, and the tiny display screen on the front had a lightning-bolt shaped crack down the middle of it. But, from Carl's experience, that wouldn't stop it from doing its job.

He flipped the phone open and pressed the power button. Sure enough, it lit up. The worn scratches on the inside screen made the display cloudy, but still readable. As Carl watched the phone boot up, he saw it access the local cell network, which meant it had an active sim card in it, and then it signed on to the hotel's wifi, which meant whoever sent it had already been in the building.

Carl went directly into the phone's directory. Sure enough, it had one phone number programmed into it; the number the cabby had given him. The Man With The Hair-Colored Hair was getting insistent.

"Son of a bitch," Carl murmured to himself.

The hotel phone on the desk rang, nearly making Carl jump out of his skin.

"Agent Abrams," Isaac's voice said as Carl picked up the phone. "Are we still in one piece?"

"We're all good," Carl said. "False alarm. Thanks for calling."

"Is this going to happen every time you get a package?" Isaac asked.

"I'm not at liberty to say," Carl said, and hung up the phone, turning his attention to the other phone.

You follow me around all day, Carl thought to himself. If you want to talk, why not just talk?

As though on cue, the phone rang. Whoever set the phone up had changed the ringtone from the factory setting to an annoyingly monotone version of "Born In The USA."

Carl let it ring for a moment, quickly looking out his window. Across the street from the hotel was a tall office building with darkened windows. It was impossible to tell if anyone was watching him from there. Peering down at the street, he saw only casual pedestrians moving through the streets. Nobody stood out as trying to look up into his room.

The phone continued to ring. It was on it's sixth round of "Born In The USA" before Carl finally gave in and pressed the answer button.

"Special Agent Carl Abrams speaking," Carl said, trying to sound as authoritative as one can to someone you can't point a gun at.

"Agent Abrams," a calm female voice responded. "We've been trying to reach you about the extended warranty on your vehicle."

Carl blinked. He'd answered the phone prepared to do his usual tough cop act; "Who do you think you are," "I'm a federal officer," blah blah blah. He immediately forgot how to do that.

Before Carl could recollect his thoughts, the voice on the other end started laughing.

"I'm sorry," she said. "I couldn't resist. How's your day been, Agent?"

"You mean besides getting a mysterious package?" Carl said. "You're harassing a federal agent, you know."

"We gave you our phone number, Carl," the woman said, her tone actually sounding like a mother admonishing her child. "I think waiting four days for you to call is being more than patient, considering what's at stake."

"Why not just come say hello?" Carl asked. "I've seen your boyfriend stalking me all over town."

"He's not stalking you," the woman said. "He's watching your back. You go out alone way too much. It worries us."

"Who exactly is 'us?'" Carl asked.

"Me and the rest of the Secret Council of Talking Animals," the woman said, and laughed at her own joke again. "I'm sorry, it's just that you're so serious, I can't help it."

Carl sighed. He wasn't sure what he should have expected from a mysterious informant in Landfall.

"Look, Carl," she continued, "we can help you, we wouldn't be here otherwise. But before we do, we need you to figure out who is standing over you."

"Standing over me?" Carl asked. "What does that even mean?"

"Like a mountain," the woman said. "An angry mountain looking down on you, waiting for you to do something it doesn't like."

"That doesn't make any sense," Carl said.

"Sometimes it doesn't make sense until it does," the woman said, as though that explained everything. It was becoming apparent to Carl this form of interrogation was not going to be productive. He needed to get whoever this was into a more controlled environment.

"If you come into police headquarters we can protect you," Carl said.

"Not likely," the woman said. "Besides, we haven't ruled any of the cops out yet."

"You think there are cops involved in this?" Carl asked.

"I don't know if I'd use the word 'involved,'" she said, sighing. She sounded as though she was just as disappointed in the answer as he was. "But that doesn't mean they're necessarily on your side."

"What makes you say that?" Carl asked.

The line was silent for a moment.

"Did you see the tattoos, Carl?" she asked. "The insignia on the hospital staff?"

Carl waited for a moment to answer. This was going exactly how he didn't want it to. Just continuing this conversation would be a gift-wrapped present to a defense lawyer if they ever found out about it. If this case all comes down to matching tattoos, then it's nothing but a government smear job against free expression.

"Yeah," Carl said. "I saw them."

"Now," the woman said, slowly, "can you tell me with

absolute certainty, that there are no cops in that office that might be...sympathetic?"

Carl knew all too well what she was talking about. Half of his job had been rooting out supremacy groups that had infiltrated local law enforcement offices. There had even been one or two Sheriffs offices in The South that unofficially made Klan membership a prerequisite for employment. It was almost a given that Landfall Police had their fair share. Carl had yet to see a local police department that was totally untouched.

"How do I know I can trust anything you say?" Carl asked. "You're just some weird lady on the phone."

"Story of my life," she said, soundly genuinely tired of being described that way. Carl got the impression she'd had this conversation many times before.

"Oh, I know! The letters!" she said suddenly. "There was no mention of the letters in the news. So, only the person who wrote the letters would even know they existed, right?"

"You wrote the letters?" Carl asked. "You're the one who started this whole damn thing?"

"Yeah," she said. "We wanted to do the cell phone thing, but we couldn't get enough together."

"If that's true," Carl said, "then you can tell me what's in the letters. Or, more importantly, you can come in for questioning and tell us how you even knew the babies were switched in the first place."

"You're really fixated on this whole 'come in for questioning' thing," she said. "I can just as easily answer your questions over the phone."

"If you really wanted to help, you'd do this through proper channels," Carl said.

"Didn't I already mention that?" the woman said,

sounding genuinely confused. "There's someone standing over you, Carl. I thought I already said that. Maybe we should start over."

"No, you did already say that," Carl asked. "It just didn't make any sense the first time either."

"Sometimes it doesn't make sense until it does," she replied.

"I'm getting a headache," Carl said. "You can't offer me any evidence and you won't come in for questioning. What is the point of any of this, then?"

"I can help," she said. "What do you need?"

"I need you to turn yourself in," Carl said. "You need to tell us how you knew the babies were switched."

"I can't do that," the woman said. "Pretend I don't exist. What would you need then?"

"Pretend you don't exist?" Carl asked. "You want me to pretend my only witness to the crime doesn't exist?"

"I'm not your only witness," she said. "Come on, think. If this was a normal case in any other city, what would you need most right now?"

"It doesn't work like that," Carl said. "I can't just wish for evidence to prove what I want to prove."

"But there are pieces missing," the woman said. "You could connect the dots if you just had another dot to connect, right?

"Just tell me how you knew the babies were stolen," Carl said. "Why is that so hard?"

"Trust me when I tell you that you don't want to know," she said. "All you need to know is that my information is mostly accurate."

"Mostly accurate?" Carl said.

"Sometimes it doesn't make sense until it does," the

woman repeated. "I can tell you that your instincts are correct, the symbol they're tattooed with is the key. Keep following that."

"My superiors aren't too keen on me taking the case in that direction," Carl said. "I've already been informed that if this involves a White Power group, then the FBIs involvement will basically evaporate."

"Well, now who's not making sense?" she said. "I don't know what to tell you. I just know that the Wolfsangel symbol is involved, which means just about anybody in that whole White Power mess could be involved."

"Again, how do you know this?" Carl asked. "If you want me to take you seriously, I need to know how you know these things."

She paused again before answering.

"It's complicated," she said. "But if it helps, I can tell you why these babies were taken."

"Go on," Carl said.

"You're an expert in these White Supremacy groups," she said. "So you know these guys pervert just about anything they can get their hands on. Mythology, superstitions, fairy tales..."

"I know what you're talking about," Carl said. "There's a reason the head of the KKK is called a 'wizard.'"

"Right," she said. "So, they're taking babies that are born from well-to-do, influential, white families, who conceived on the night of the full moon."

"Excuse me?" Carl said.

"That's what all the babies have in common," she said. "They were all conceived on a full moon."

"That's fucking crazy," Carl said. "How would anyone even fucking know that?"

There was another moment of silence on her end.

"Oh, right," she said finally. "You're a guy, so you don't know. Carl, when a woman gets pregnant, hospitals get all up in our business. They want to know when our last period was, how often we have sex, how many partners we've had in our life, and so on, and so on. It's embarrassing how obsessed they get with us. But with all that, they can narrow down when a baby was conceived within a couple of days, and they put it right in it's own easy-to-find square in your file. Anyone with access to hospital records can see the conception date of any baby that might be born in their maternity ward. If that falls within a full moon phase, that's who they target."

"Jesus Christ," Carl said.

"I know, right." she responded.

"You said you're not a hospital employee," Carl said.

"That's right," she said.

"So how did you get their hospital records?" Carl asked.

"I've never seen their hospital records," she said.

"Then how do you even know this?" Carl said.

"If you look into it yourself," she said, "you'll see that I'm right. That's really all you need to do."

Carl sighed. He was relatively sure there was no legal way for him to confirm what she was saying, but there was no point in getting into that with her.

"What does the full moon have to do with it?" Carl asked. "Why do they want kids conceived on the full moon?"

"Superstition," she said. "They've latched on to some random medieval belief that says these kids will have special powers or something."

"So you're saying," Carl said, "that we're dealing with a Neo-Nazi cult, that's infiltrated an entire hospital network, in order to kidnap kids that they think will grow up to be super-nazis?"

"And they would've gotten away with it too," she said, "if it weren't for us lousy kids."

"I can't go down this road," Carl said. "This is exactly what my superiors told me not to go digging for. If I chase this theory, I'm not just off the case; I might even be fired."

"Not if it's true," she said. "If we're right, you get the 'I Told You So' Of The Year Award."

"And you're going to refuse to tell me how you know all this," Carl grumbled. "The two of you just put all of this together on your own without any hospital records or evidence."

"Three of us," the woman said. "But yes, that's pretty much what happened."

"Who's the third person?" Carl asked.

"My other boyfriend," the woman said. "They're both keeping an eye on you for me. They're good boys."

That was the first bit of truly shocking information that Carl had gotten from this woman. There was a second person following him that he hadn't seen. Perhaps that was why Mr. Grumpy-Face was standing out so deliberately; to focus Carl's attention away from anyone who might have gotten even closer to him. The thought of it made the hairs on his neck stand up.

"Can't you give me anything concrete to go on?" Carl said, "As much as I'd love to, I can't just start hauling Nazis in for questioning. I need probable cause."

Carl hoped he hadn't taken too long to change the subject. The last thing he needed was to spook whoever the second guy was. Now that he knows to look for him, Carl might actually be able to get his hands on the "other boyfriend."

"I'm sorry," she said. "That's not how this works. Maybe I'll have something new in the morning."

"Why the morning?" Carl asked. "What's happening tonight?"

"Oh, I probably shouldn't tell you," she said. "You don't want to get a reputation."

"I'm already regretting this entire conversation," Carl said.

"Can I ask you something?" she said, her voice suddenly sounding timid.

"Sure, you can ask," Carl said.

"The other babies," she said. "The ones with the...that were left behind. I can't...I don't know anything about them. Where they've come from, or where they're going. Can you tell me if they're okay?"

"They've been taken by Child Services," Carl said. It wasn't exactly privileged information, so there was no harm in telling her. It even helped Carl to feel a little better about it to say it out loud himself. "Some of the victims' families have already offered to adopt them, but it's not as simple as all that. In the long term, I'm sure they're going to be fine."

"That's good," she sounded genuinely relieved. "I'm glad to hear it. Good luck, Agent."

With that, the line went dead.

Carl looked down at the phone. With all its scuffs and cracks, it had performed its duty flawlessly. They don't make them like this anymore.

He thought for a moment about calling Burgess. There was a lot to talk about now, the package not being a bomb notwithstanding. Carl settled for sending a text for now. They could have the conversation in the morning. Burgess would want to have his people run down the origins of the phone anyway.

Carl was pretty sure that he wouldn't be able to sleep that night. After such a twisted interaction, how could he not spend the whole night staring at the ceiling and trying to make sense of it? But, as he discovered, there was a certain point where the nonsense his brain tried to make sense simply short-circuited the whole process and he passed out from the exhaustion of even trying. He wasn't even aware of any passage of time between his head hitting the pillow and his alarm jerking him awake.

As he rose from bed, a light caught the corner of his eye. He turned to see the recycled cell phone sitting on the table next to the bed. A tiny, but impressively bright light was flashing on it, indicating that he'd received a text.

Carl flipped open the phone to read the message from the mysterious weird girl.

The message was a set of GPS coordinates and one sentence; "Bring cadaver dogs."

CHAPTER FIVE
LOST IN THE WILDERNESS

"What was that you were saying about anonymous tips?" Burgess asked.

The two of them stood at the edge of the trail as uniformed officers strung Crime Scene tape around the trees. The City Parks official followed them around, dutifully making sure none of them stepped on anything they weren't supposed to.

Wilderness Park was over five-thousand acres of protected land, hugging right up against downtown Landfall. It was a beloved site for hiking, cycling, and even horseback riding, but stepping off the trails meant bringing down the wrath of the only people in Landfall that were less fun than the police; The Parks Department. It was the perfect place to hide a body, if you had gigantic brass balls.

Sure enough, the cadaver dogs found an unmarked grave a hundred yards off a lesser-used trail, right where the GPS coordinates said it would be. Police lab techs were taking their time digging it up, shifting every bit of earth as carefully as they could. Carl had to respect the extra care they were putting forth for the preservation of the crime scene, but he couldn't help but notice how often the techs were looking over their shoulders at the City Parks Officials.

"Did you get anything off the trace?" Carl asked, ignoring Burgess' question.

"The phone is a relic," Burgess said. "The original owner donated it to a recycling center in Texas four years ago. The sim card is from a prepaid reseller in Chicago. They buy them by the gross."

"They don't keep track of who they're sold to?" Carl asked.

"Not if they pay cash," Burgess said.

"You've got to be fucking kidding me," Carl said.

"You think your girl actually road-tripped around the country to get an untraceable phone?" Burgess asked.

"She wouldn't have to," Carl said. "These days you can get it all online. You don't even have to go on the dark web."

"Except," Burgess pointed out, "Your girl said she couldn't muster up enough phones for the families. That's why she sent the letters."

"Good point," Carl said. "So she's paranoid enough that she had to find them in person and pay cash."

"I don't even know any drug dealers that are that paranoid," Burgess said. "Who do you think she's hiding from?"

"Besides us?" Carl said.

"Naturally," Burgess said.

"The Sokolov Brothers, maybe?" Carl said.

"Say again?" Burgess said.

"Leon at the Cajun cart recognized my stalker," Carl said. "Said he didn't know his name, but he was definitely the guy who ran the Sokolovs into traffic."

"That's weird," Burgess said. "Leon knows everybody's name."

"Can you think of any other cases like that?" Carl asked. "Some 'normal looking dude' stirring up shit and vanishing?"

Burgess was quiet as he thought that one over.

"About six months ago," he said. "We got a report of a sort of car-jacking."

"A 'sort of' car-jacking?" Carl asked.

"A guy calls in to say he'd been car-jacked," Burgess explains. "When the unis get there, the guy is just sitting there on the sidewalk with his car sitting in the middle of the road, blocking traffic."

"Okay?" Carl said.

"He says he'd stopped at the intersection when somebody knocked on his window," Burgess said. "He rolled his window down just enough to hear what the guy had to say, and the guy tells him to get out of the car."

"Did he have a weapon," Carl asked.

"Nope," Burgess said. "Just a real stern tone of voice. So, the victim tells him to fuck off, and, get this, the guy grabs the car window and rips it out."

"The hell?" Carl said.

"He grabs the top of the window and pulls," Burgess said. "The window just shatters right out of the car door."

"I didn't even know you could do that," Carl said.

"I'd never heard of it before," Burgess said. "So, the dude reaches into the car, opens the door, and hauls the victim out. He doesn't hurt him or nothing. He just plants him on his ass on the sidewalk. He then goes back to the car, rips all of the ignition wires out from under the dash, and walks off with them."

"That's it?" Carl said.

"That's it," Burgess said. "Just stranded the motherfucker right in the middle of the street."

"That doesn't make any sense," Carl said.

"Well, stop the presses," Burgess said.

"And I take it the victim couldn't give a detailed description?" Carl asked.

"Get this," Burgess said, "he couldn't make a description at all."

"What?" Carl said.

"The victim was almost seventy years old," Burgess said, "and apparently he'd forgotten his glasses at home. He couldn't see a damn thing."

"But," Carl said, "he was driving a car."

"You noticed that too, huh?" Burgess said.

Carl was quiet for a moment.

"Am I crazy," Carl said, "or did that guy maybe save a life that day?"

"The Waterfront Music Festival was going on that weekend," Burgess said, grimly. "He might've saved a few lives."

"Did he get cut when he broke the window?" Carl asked.

"Sure did," Burgess said. "We've got the sample in evidence, but the department doesn't want to spend the money on a DNA test until we have a suspect to match it to."

"Of course," Carl frowned.

"May not've been the same guy, though," Burgess said.

"Yeah," Carl said, sarcastically. "I'm sure they're totally unrelated."

"How do you figure the girl fits into all this?" Burgess asked.

"From the way she talks," Carl said, "sounds like she's the

one in charge."

"You think she's the one telling him to run into traffic and slap around old men?" Burgess said.

"She's definitely the one who told him to follow me around," Carl said.

"And there's another one out there somewhere?" Burgess said.

"A second boyfriend," Carl nodded. "Good for her, honestly."

"Any idea what his role is in this?" Burgess asked.

"Nope," Carl said. "but I suppose somebody had to drive around the country to pay cash for an untraceable phone."

"This doesn't sound like a healthy relationship to me," Burgess said.

Just then, one of the Crime Scene Techs waved over at them from the dig site.

"We're ready for you, Lieutenant," the tech called out.

Seemingly from nowhere, a City Parks Official suddenly appeared next to Carl.

"Gentlemen," he said, startling Carl. "Please follow directly behind me, and step where I step. Thank you."

Carl rolled his eyes and did as instructed. The three of them marched carefully through the brush until they came to the cleared out plot of ground that had already been tread flat by the lab techs, encircling a hole dug out of the ground. At the bottom of the hole, a body was partially uncovered. The techs were still working diligently to uncover the rest of it without disturbing any possible evidence, but they'd uncovered enough for Carl to see that it was the body of a young boy, barely a teenager.

"He's been down there about six months, give or take a couple weeks," one of the techs said. "Male, Caucasian, somewhere between thirteen and fourteen years old."

"Christ," Burgess cursed. "Have you found what killed him yet?"

"He's got a lot of pretty bad injuries," the tech said. "Bruises, claw marks, blunt force trauma in multiple locations. Don't know which of them finally got him, but it looks like he lost a fight with a wild animal."

"What kind of animal?" Carl asked.

"Don't know for sure, yet" the tech said. "Won't know til we get him back to the lab."

"Anything down there with the body," Burgess asked.

"Nothing so far," the tech said. "Not even any clothes. Looks like some of his teeth were pulled out too."

"His teeth?" Carl said.

"His incisors, to be exact," the tech said.

"Agent Abrams," Burgess said, "have you ever heard of a wild animal that pulls out incisors?"

"I have not, Lieutenant Burgess," Carl said.

"As fascinating as this is," Burgess said, "what does this have to do with our missing kids?"

"Well," Carl said, kneeling closer to the edge of the hole and withdrawing a laser pointer from his pocket. "Could you clear off this section of the body, please."

Another lab tech that was still in the hole looked down at where Carl's laser was indicating. The tech nodded and carefully began brushing away the dirt on the body's chest.

"You carry a laser pointer around?" Burgess asked.

"You don't?" Carl responded. "How do you point at something in a hole?"

Burgess demonstrated by pointing his finger into the hole.

"That's as clean as I can get it," the lab tech in the hole

called out.

The body was bloated and discolored, but it didn't take much imagination to see the Wolfsangel symbol tattooed on the victim's chest, just below the collarbone.

"What's that look like to you, Lieutenant?" Carl asked.

"Looks like he's late for his shift at the hospital," Burgess said.

"Is it enough to bring in suspects for questioning?" Carl said.

"I'll talk to the D.A.," Burgess said, "but we're probably going to have to confirm an ID on the kid first."

"Call me when you've got something," Carl said, "I've seen all I want to see here."

"Where are you going?" Burgess asked.

"I'm done with this Daytime TV sneak-around bullshit," Carl said. "I'm going to go arrest my stalker and find out how his girlfriend knew where a body was buried."

"You sure you don't want backup?" Burgess asked.

"He only shows his face when I'm alone," Carl said, marching back through the brush to the hiking path. "Don't worry, I've got this."

"If you say so," Burgess called back to him. "Remember to look both ways."

* * *

Carl must've strolled through the entirety of downtown Landfall three times before he felt like giving up. The cab he'd taken from the edge of Wilderness Park dropped him off in front of the police station, and from there he wandered through the city, taking the time to pause at his usual places; Leon's cart, the hotel, the coffee shop between Leon's cart and the station, etc. All the while glancing at every window he passed in order to check the reflection for any sign as to who Mr. Grumpy-face's partner might be.

It was an infuriating practice. The stalker was there from the moment Carl stepped out of the cab. For blocks upon blocks, every time Carl glanced at the view behind him, the perpetually scowling face was a hundred paces behind him with no sign of any other recurring face. Whoever this "other boyfriend" was, he was invisible.

It occurred to Carl that he might have gotten it wrong, and Frowny-Face was the close-up man, while the second guy had more of an eagle-eye perch somewhere. So, Carl shifted his strategy, moving into tightly packed walkways between buildings, trying to coax the Hair-Colored Hair Guy into any position where he couldn't easily disappear if Carl turned on him. But that was like playing a game of checkers with only two pieces.

Carl actually felt himself getting tired after a while, and on his fourth passing of his favorite local coffee shop, he decided to go in for a coffee this time.

It took Carl ten minutes to work through the line and collect his coffee and muffin. Sitting at a table that put his back to an unoccupied corner of the shop, he looked out the front windows of the coffee shop to see his stalker standing across the street, casually leaning against a wall and glaring back at Carl.

"Not my fault your job sucks," Carl muttered.

Carl had finished his muffin and was halfway finished with his coffee when he started to lose patience.

Not really sure what his plan was, Carl pulled the archaic cell phone from his pocket and pressed the Call button on its one stored number.

The phone rang, but went to voicemail.

"Just because you have my number," the recording of the girl's voice said, "doesn't mean I have to talk to you. Leave a message."

Carl scoffed and pressed the End Call button, then dialed again, getting the voicemail a second time.

Carl glanced out the window again. The Scowl hadn't moved. Not even a little. He stood there, his against a concrete building, like some sort of angry art installation.

Nobody else on the street was stopping, so if the partner was around, he'd be in the coffee shop with Carl. But Carl was almost certain that nobody had entered the shop after him.

Carl dialed the number a third time. This time the line clicked on and a real voice answered.

"Stop looking at me, Carl" a male voice said. "You'll blow my cover."

Carl blinked. His stalker still hadn't moved, still hadn't even stopped scowling. His hands were stuffed in his coat pockets, and Carl realized he must have the phone in one of those pockets and a wireless earpiece.

"You're my tour guide, I take it?" Carl said. "Where's your girlfriend?"

"Not here," the stalker said.

Mr. Frowny-Face remained motionless, glaring at Carl from across the street. From that distance, Carl couldn't even be sure his lips were moving when he spoke.

"Look," Carl said. "You're already in serious enough trouble. You've been stalking me since I got into town, you're withholding information about a mass kidnapping, and now you apparently know something about the death of a minor that was illegally disposed of. If you and your girlfriend don't turn yourselves in for questioning now, you're going to be charged as accessories when we catch you."

There was a long silence. The stalker wasn't responding, and Carl started to feel like he was deliberately goading him into some kind of long-distance staring contest.

"This is your last chance," Carl said. "Come in here and talk to me, or I put out a bulletin to have every cop in town pick you up."

"Too dangerous," the stalker said.

"I trust the lieutenant I'm working with," Carl said. "He can make sure nothing happens to you in custody."

"Not for me," he said. "For you."

"You think I'm in danger?" Carl said.

"Someone's standing over you," the stalker said. "Until we know who it is, we can't make ourselves known."

"Your girlfriend mentioned that before," Carl said. "What's that supposed to even mean?"

Silence again.

"Look," Carl said. "Can you at least tell me your name? I'm tired of calling you The Hair-Colored Hair Guy."

This clearly took The Local aback. Even from across the street, Carl could see him blink in surprise. His face didn't look any more or less angry, though.

"Why the fuck would you call me that?" he said.

"I don't know," Carl said. "I heard someone say that and it stuck. Work with me here. What can I call you?"

He didn't answer right away, but Carl could tell it wasn't the usual stand off. The sound of a deep breath came through the phone as the stalker considered Carl's request.

"Walter," he said finally.

"Your name is Walter?" Carl said.

"As far as you're concerned," Walter said.

"Okay, that's something, I suppose," Carl said. "Walter, this is serious stuff. I got the location of a dead body from you. Which means, failing any other evidence, that makes you a subject of a murder investigation. The longer you avoid questioning, the worse it's going to be for you."

"You don't need us for that, Carl," Walter said. "We just gave you the lead."

"You gave me a body," Carl said. "All that does is raise more questions."

"Yes," Walter said. "But they're the right questions now. You said you needed a connection between the Wolfsangel tattoo and the missing kids. Now you have one."

"I have a Wolfsangel tattoo on a dead body," Carl said. "How does that connect to the missing babies?"

"I'm here to watch your back, Carl," Walter said. "Not do your job for you."

Carl felt his phone vibrate in his pocket. That's what he was waiting for.

Taking care to keep his phone from where "Walter" might notice it from his vantage point, Carl glanced down at the screen. His plan had worked.

While ordering his coffee, Carl had slipped a ten dollar bill and a note to the barista. A few minutes later, the barista stepped outside for a smoke break and managed to snap a photo of "Walter" without being noticed, sending it immediately to Carl's phone.

"What do you expect me to do, Walter?" Carl said, drawing out the conversation as long as he could. "Violate civil liberties by arresting everyone in town with a Wolfsangel tattoo?"

Carl had long since found the value of being able to send

texts without looking at his phone, and had been practicing doing so for years. The photo was off to Burgess in a matter of seconds.

"Don't pretend like it didn't occur to you, Deep State," Walter replied. "Just keep doing what you do, and you'll get it."

Carl could feel his teeth grind. It wasn't the first time a perp had called him "Deep State." It had gotten so common that even some of his colleagues at The Bureau had started calling him that. That didn't make it any less annoying, but this was not the time to get annoyed.

"What I do," Carl said, "is question suspects, which is what you are right now."

"No I'm not," Walter replied. "I'm just a guy."

"A guy who fed me the location of a dead body," Carl said.

"You can't prove that," Walter said. "You can't even prove I'm on the phone with you right now. The most solid lead you have is a body that has the same tattoo as the hospital staff. And once you ID the body, you'll have everything you need."

Carl's phone vibrated again with a response from Burgess; the nearest squad car was only two minutes away.

"I feel like we're going in circles here, Carl," Walter said, sighing. "Finish your coffee and go back to the station so I can go home."

"Where's the girl?" Carl said, keeping Walter's attention on him. "Let me talk to her, since she's clearly the one in charge."

"I already told you," Walter said. "She's not here."

"Where is she?" Carl pushed. "Out murdering another teenager?"

Walter didn't respond immediately. Carl wasn't expecting any kind of confession. He didn't actually think they had anything to do with the body, but most people can't help but blurt out relevant information if it's to try and prove someone wrong. Throwing out blatantly incorrect statements is one of the oldest interrogation techniques, right next to just smacking somebody around.

"You're upset," Walter said calmly. "I get it. When she's feeling better, I'll have her call you. She can tell you what a great job you're doing."

Feeling better? Carl wondered. *Is she sick? Injured?*

"You know," Carl said. "For someone who claims to be one of the good guys, you're kind of an asshole."

Silence again. Carl didn't really need "Walter" to lose his temper. He just needed him to stay in one spot for one more minute.

"You're right," Walter said, to Carl's surprise. "I'm sorry. We appreciate your help. We couldn't do this without you."

It was Carl's turn to be silent. He'd never had a suspect apologize to him before. He was almost certain there was nothing about that in the FBI Handbook.

"Or," Walter added a beat later, "so I'm told."

Asshole.

"Listen, this might just be a fun little video game to you..." Carl started to say.

"Fuck," Walter blurted suddenly. "Dammit, Carl!"

With that, the line went dead, and Carl watched as Walter bolted down the street. A second later, a squad car rolled past the coffee shop, it's lights rolling as they pursued Walter.

Carl frowned and dialed Burgess.

"Did we get him?" Burgess answered.

"The unis fucked it up," Carl said. "He saw them coming

and took off."

"Well, don't worry," Burgess said. "I'm sure they'll catch up to him. You better get back to the station. Things got a little hinky with the body."

"You didn't lose it, did you?" Carl joked.

"We don't lose bodies in Landfall," Burgess said, with enough rehearsed authority that it was definitely something he's had to say a lot.

* * *

Dr. Conrad, the city's Medical Examiner, led Burgess and Carl into the morgue with a file folder waving around in her hand as she spoke.

"This is my own personal phobia come to life," she said. "I've had nightmares about this since I was a kid."

"About this specifically?" Burgess asked.

"No, not this specifically," Conrad said. "But close enough. Doing this examination wasn't fun for me."

"Is it usually fun?" Carl asked.

"Usually it's like I get to go to Science Camp every day," Conrad said, spinning on her heels to face Carl. "You ruined that with your creepy forest body."

She spun back around and circled around the body laid out on the exam table.

"Why is this my fault?" Carl whimpered.

"It sure as shit isn't my fault," Burgess said.

"Jump to the end," Conrad said, opening the file folder as she stood over the body, "is that he died of blood loss. Not for lack of trying, though. He has bruises everywhere, one foot had broken bones, his shoulder was dislocated, and he had bite and claw marks basically everywhere, including his face."

"Holy crap," Carl said.

"But that's not all," Conrad announced, with all the gravitas of a game show announcer. "It wasn't the first time. I found healed over wounds as well. Cuts and bites that were several days old before death, and one of his arms had been broken and reset twice before. Whoever killed this kid had tried to kill him a half-dozen times before."

"I'm confused," Burgess said. "You keep suggesting he was killed by a 'who,' but you mentioned claw marks. That suggests he was killed by a 'what.'"

"Look at you," Conrad cooed, "homicide detective and grammar police, all in one."

Burgess grimaced but didn't respond.

"Measurement of the claw marks suggest he was attacked by a wolf," Conrad said. "However, depending on which claw mark you look at, it's a different kind of wolf. This one here, for instance, matches a Northwestern Timber Wolf, while this one right next to it is from an Alaskan Tundra Wolf."

"Okay, that's weird," Carl said.

"Not if he was killed by a person," Conrad said. "You can buy wolf claws on the black market. I don't imagine there's a lot of quality control involved to make sure you have a matching set, them being sadistic criminals and all."

"So, someone made a weapon with a bunch of wolf claws on it and beat this kid with it?" Burgess said.

"My job is to give you the factual data, not make guesses," Conrad said. "But, yeah, that's my guess."

"You said there were bite marks as well?" Carl asked.

"From multiple species' of wolves as well," Conrad said. "This bite mark here has teeth from three different kinds of wolves in the set."

"Seems like a particularly cruel way to kill someone," Burgess said. "Were there defensive wounds or signs of restraints?"

"All over the place," Conrad said. "A majority of the wounds, including the partially healed ones, were on his forearms. But we've also got uniformed bruising around his wrists and fingers, like something tight was wrapped around each knuckle."

"The crime scene techs said he had teeth missing," Carl said.

"His top two incisors," Conrad nodded. "They were pulled out postmortem. Basically, he got into a fight with this wolf-weapon person six, maybe seven times over the span of three years. I'd say he died about an hour after the last fight, and then his teeth were pulled out a few minutes after that."

"Maybe some kind of wolf-themed fight club?" Carl said. "The White Power crowd is big on ultra machismo."

"Taking trophies, though?" Burgess thought out loud. "That doesn't seem like their style. Not of their own kind, at least."

"I think we're already past the usual MO," Carl said. "They're taking the Werewolf theme way further than I would've expected. Even the actual Nazis only used it as a nickname."

"Okay," Burgess said, "the dead kid with a White Power tattoo definitely means we can start questioning people with the same tattoo. But it isn't enough to arrest any of them, and it certainly doesn't connect to the missing kids in any way that would satisfy your bosses."

"Did we get an ID on him?" Carl asked.

"Nothing," Conrad said. "Fingerprints didn't get any hits,

dental records were a no go, and his face is too messed up to even try matching him to any missing persons."

"Well, we could try reconstructing his face from x-rays of his skull," Carl said. "But I doubt I could get my superiors to agree to that, since I don't have a good reason to connect him to my case."

"Any way we could get a DNA match?" Burgess asked.

"The kid is fifteen years old," Conrad snorted. "There's no way his DNA is on file anywhere. The best we could hope for is to send it into one of those heredity sites and maybe in a few weeks we can find a relative, if we're lucky."

"We're open to suggestions," Burgess said to Conrad. "If this kid is connected to our case, we need to know who he is."

"Well," Conrad said, "how'd you find him in the first place?"

Burgess and Carl glanced nervously at each other.

"Anonymous tip," Carl confessed.

"Oh, well, that's fuckin' useless," Conrad said.

"Alright," Burgess said, "How long until you finish the full report. I'm going to need that before I can take this to a judge."

"Tomorrow afternoon," Conrad said. "Assuming nobody else dies."

"Better than nothing, I guess," Burgess said. "We can start pulling in the Nazi Nurses for questioning then."

"Nazi Nurses," Conrad said. "I can't wait to hear how this story ends."

* * *

Two uniformed officers were waiting in Burgess' office.

One of them was holding an ice pack to the back of his head and neither of them looked like they wanted to talk about it.

"Where's our mystery man?" Burgess asked them as he approached. Carl assumed that must mean they were the unis that were sent to chase after Walter.

Neither of them said anything. They just looked sheepishly at each other.

"Are you fucking kidding me?" Burgess responded to their silence.

"There is something seriously weird about that guy," the first one said. The second, with the ice pack, just shook his head in disbelief.

"What happened?" Carl asked.

"I chased him down on Pine Avenue," the first cop said. "Ronnie managed to circle around Second to get in front of him. He ran right into him at the corner of Ash."

"I hit him with my taser," the second cop, presumably Ronnie, said. "But he didn't stop."

"He didn't stop?" Carl said. "With a taser on him?"

"You sure you hit skin?" Burgess asked. "Did your taser misfire?"

"Naw," Ronnie said, looking at the floor. "I got him."

"So what happened?" Burgess pressed, his voice getting louder.

"He grabbed me," Ronnie said. "He grabbed my hands while the taser was still on. He just kept running at me and grabbed my hands. He did it so fast, it was like..."

Ronnie didn't finish his sentence. He just looked at the floor like he was questioning every decision he'd ever made in life.

Carl suddenly felt very sorry for Ronnie. He'd seen what happens when a perp getting tazed makes contact with the one holding the tazer. They both end up getting electrocuted, and the one holding the taser can't let go. In training they tell you to stay at least ten feet away before firing the weapon, so that it doesn't end up accidentally killing you both.

"Fuck," Carl said, in solidarity.

"I dropped like a bag of rocks," Ronnie said, shamefully. "But he stayed standing somehow. He just pulled the taser out of my hands as I fell and ran off with it."

"He ran off with your taser?" Burgess shouted.

"Wires were still stuck in his chest," the first cop said. "He barely even slowed down."

"How the hell is that even possible?" Carl asked.

"Go get yourself to the infirmary and get checked out," Burgess said to Ronnie. "After that, get back down to Pine and see if anyone has any security footage of what happened. See if we can't trace where he went from there."

The two officers nodded and shuffled out of Burgess' office.

"What is even up with this guy?" Burgess said in exasperation. "Who the fuck can stay standing with fifty-thousand volts running through him? That shit ain't human!"

"I'm going to make a phone call," Carl said, as casually as possible, and turned to leave.

"You tell that little shit that I'm coming for him," Burgess shouted as Carl headed for the elevators. "This city ain't big enough to hide from me!"

* * *

Once outside, Carl dialed the relic phone and looked up and down the street as the line rang.

"You're a real dick, Carl," Walter said as he answered.

"You assaulted a police officer," Carl spat back. "You are so fucked now."

"He startled me," Walter said. "Tell him I said I'm sorry."

"You're sorry?" Carl laughed. "Tell him yourself when he's arresting you."

"Carl, let's take a breath here," Walter said. "We're all the good guys. We should be working together."

"Turn yourself in, and we can do that," Carl said.

"I've already told you why I can't do that," Walter replied.

"All you have done," Carl said slowly, "is fuck up my case. Turn yourself in, and we can talk about this like adults. But if we have to come arrest you, I'm going to pin the dead body to you."

"Goddammit, Carl," Walter said. "Will you just ID the body, already? We'll be out of each others' hair by the weekend."

"We can't ID the body!" Carl shouted. "There's no connection to the hospital except for the stupid tattoo, and that's nothing!"

Walter was silent for a moment.

"What do you mean, you can't ID the body?" Walter said, slowly.

"I mean, we can't ID the body," Carl said. "Nothing comes up. Fingerprints, dental records, there isn't even anything from missing persons that matches him even close. He's a total nobody. His tombstone will say 'John Doe.'"

"But that's..." Walter started. "That usually works."

"What works?" Carl pressed.

"You said you needed a connection between the tattoo and the missing kids," Walter said. "That was supposed to be it."

"Says who?" Carl asked. "How did you know that body

was there?"

Walter went quiet again. Longer this time.

"Carl," he said, "I'm going to have to call you back."

"Don't you dare hang up on me!" Carl shouted. "You and your girlfriend need to get your asses to the station and explain yourselves."

"You want us to turn ourselves in?" Walter said. "Then you need to make sure we can do that without tipping our hand."

"What's that supposed to mean?" Carl said.

"Someone is standing over you," Walter said sharply. "Find out who."

With that, the line went dead.

Carl barely managed to stop himself from throwing the phone into traffic.

CHAPTER SIX
BRIGHT LIGHTS, SMALL CITY

The first of the Nazi Nurses they got into an interrogation room was Paulie Vance. It had turned out to be something of a blessing that they could honestly say there was no known connection between the body in the woods and the missing infants. This meant they were able to send uniformed officers to collect their People of Interest without any interference from the hospital legal team.

In Carl's mind, Paulie Vance looked like an asshole. If he was casting a movie, and needed an obvious asshole character, the casting company would send Paulie Vance without even thinking about it. He looked that much like an asshole.

Paulie was lean and wiry, and had a genetically permanent smug look on his face. His hair was blond, like a good little Nazi, but rather than being cut short into some pseudo-military flat-top, he wore it close-cropped to the side of his head with an obvious side-part of the longer hair on top. That, paired with a well-groomed handlebar mustache made him look less like a White Supremacist, and more like a member of an old-timey barbershop quartet. This was what caught Carl's attention in the first round of questioning at the hospital; Old-Timey Barbershop Asshole was the hot new look for Neo-Nazis. If not for that, Carl might not have been on alert enough to have noticed the slight edge of tattoo ink peeking out from under Paulie's sleeve. Paulie was all-too happy to show off his Vintage Nazi tattoo to the Jewish Fed that couldn't do anything about it. A classic Old-Timey Barbershop Asshole move.

As the second interrogation at the station began, Carl had to fiercely remind himself not to throw it in Paulie's face that his hubris is the only reason anyone is connecting a dead body to him and his asshole friends. As much fun as that would be, it might ruin the hope that he'll do something equally stupid again.

"Tell us about your tattoo," Burgess began, taking the lead.

Paulie didn't respond. He just smirked at them, as though they'd fallen into his clever trap. Typical Barbershop Asshole.

"We know it's a Nazi tattoo," Burgess continued. "Some sort of Aryan Dog Lovers club, right?"

Paulie's eyes narrowed in disapproval, but he didn't take the bait.

"We know there's a bunch of you working at the hospitals," Burgess pressed. "We've got more coming in right now to talk with us, just like you."

"On what grounds?" Paulie finally spoke up.

"A murder investigation," Carl interjected.

That had an effect. Paulie twitched when Carl spoke. Carl couldn't be sure if it was the gravity of the word "murder," or if Paulie was so deep into the White Supremacy rhetoric that he actually had a physical reaction to being spoken to by a Jew.

"What murder?" Paulie asked, indignant.

Without saying anything, Burgess opened the file folder with the crime scene photos and laid three of them out in a row on the table. Paulie's eyes got wider with each one.

He's one of yours," Burgess said, pointing to the clearest view of the boy's tattoo. "We thought you might want to help us find out who did this to him."

Paulie glared at the photos. He was working hard not to react to them, which was a tell in and of itself. Carl could see a mixture of anger and bewilderment in his eyes as his gaze darted to each picture.

"I don't know who that is," Paulie said through his teeth.

"You're lying," Carl said. "You expect us to believe it's just a coincidence? That you got drunk one night and woke up with matching tattoos? That kid was fourteen years old. He didn't get that at a tattoo parlor, and neither did you."

"I'm leaving," Paulie said, standing up.

"Look," Burgess said, standing as well, "we just want to help you."

"I don't need help from you," Paulie said, punching out his words to make sure they knew what he meant by "you."

"Or, you," he said to Carl, with matching venom. "Charge me with something or let me go."

"Can you just tell us his name?" Burgess said. "We can find who did this. Just tell us the kid's name."

"I don't know him," Paulie said, and circled around the table toward the door. He glared at Carl as he did, daring him to try and stop him.

Neither of them did. He was right that they didn't have any reason to hold him, and trying to keep him from leaving would only make things worse. All they could do was watch him walk out of the station, fists clenched like he was holding back the urge to break into a run.

"That was unhelpful," Burgess said.

"Plainclothes are ready to tail him?" Carl asked.

"Already got one watching his apartment," Burgess said. "Another waiting outside to make sure he actually goes home."

"That's all we can do for now," Carl said. "Maybe the next one will go better."

* * *

The next one did not go better.

Nor the next.

Each of the Wolfsangel-marked hospital staff marched into the station, looked at the photos and left. Each of them looking more angry than the first.

That's what really got to Carl; the anger. When they saw the pictures of the body, they weren't disgusted, or scared, or shocked. They were angry. Carl couldn't make sense of it.

By the time the last one stomped out of the station, it was almost 10 O' Clock. The floor had mostly emptied out and only a few lights were on for the janitorial staff. Carl and Burgess sat in Burgess' office, sipping coffee and trying to make sense of it all.

"They wouldn't even tell us his name," Burgess said in wonderment. "I've dealt with gangs before. Lots of folks will stay quiet about what they know so they can get revenge before we get to them. But I've never had them not even give us a name. You'd think they'd want us to give him a proper burial, at least."

"I get the feeling they didn't like him very much," Carl said, staring at a blank wall above Burgess' desk.

"How do you figure?" Burgess asked.

"Like Doc Conrad said," Carl said. "He'd lost a lot of fights before he got killed. Maybe they saw him as weak."

"Weak?" Burgess said in disbelief.

"Nazis are really into weeding out undesirables," Carl said. "Euthanizing the disabled, executing the failures. They might've won the war if they weren't so big on killing their own people for not measuring up."

"Well, Nazis gonna Nazi," Burgess said, shrugging.

"How the hell does this kid connect to the hospitals, though?" Carl went on. "My stalker friend was insistent that this kid was the key."

"You're still giving credit to anything that guy says?" Burgess asked.

"He knew where the body was buried," Carl said. "Like, *exactly* where it was buried. I'd be surprised if the people who buried him could be that precise."

"How do you know he wasn't the one who buried him?" Burgess asked.

"I guess I don't," Carl said. "But it makes even less sense if he did."

"I just don't get how folks get mixed up in this shit to begin with," Burgess said. "I mean, gangs I get. You grow up in the wrong neighborhood, it's either join a gang or be a victim of one. But this White Supremacy shit? How does anybody listen to that crazy Nazi shit and think it makes sense?"

"Oh, don't worry," Carl said. "They don't."

"Say again?" Burgess asked.

"They don't believe it," Carl said. "They just say they do."

"You're fucking with me?" Burgess said.

Carl shook his head and sipped his coffee.

"It's like the schoolyard bully," Carl said, "When the teacher asks him why he hit you, he says you looked at him funny. He knows it's bullshit. He just says that to fuck with you even more. Same goes for the Klan."

"That doesn't make sense," Burgess said.

"It doesn't make sense to you or me," Carl said. "But that's the point. As long as we keep assuming this is just some misunderstanding, then we won't take any real action to stop them. We'll keep trying to impress upon them the value of civility, and they'll keep kicking us in the balls for fun."

"So what?" Burgess asked. "You're saying we should just shoot them?"

"As an officer of the law," Carl said, "I would never say that. What I'm saying is that these fuckers are evil, they know they're evil, and they like being evil. Anything they say to the contrary is a bald-faced lie.

"For example," Carl continued, sitting upright suddenly, "take the original Nazi Werewolves. Their job was to blend in with normal folk, then turn into chaotic psychopaths when the time was right. That's why they called themselves Werewolves, because they knew they were monsters masquerading as humans. From Day One, they've always known what they were. They didn't actually think Jews or Communists were conspiring against Germany, or any of that shit. That was just the Nazi equivalent of 'he looked at me funny,' and they thought it was hilarious that people were falling over themselves trying to refute made-up arguments. It's like trying to tell fans of that 'you might be a redneck' comedian that rednecks aren't really like that."

"You're blowing my mind over here," Burgess said.

"So, to answer your question," Carl said, "nobody gets convinced they're the superior race. They just decide they are to fuck with you."

"So what do we do about them?" Burgess asked.

"Like I said," Carl said, grimly. "I'm an officer of the law."

The two of them sat in silence, the quiet of the empty station rolling into the office.

The two of them fell so deeply into thought, the ding from the elevator actually made them both jump.

They were about to laugh off their paranoia, when they saw the monsters step onto the floor.

They stood almost seven feet tall on sets of aluminum running stilts, fur lined straps connecting them to their feet and running in spirals up their legs. Matching straps wrapped around their shoulders and arms, leading to metal hand braces with mismatched wolf claws attached to each finger. Their heads were covered with helmets shaped like a wolf's head, articulating jaws holding rows of mismatched teeth. Their real eyes glared out from inside the masks, seeming to shoot fire of fury and hatred.

The male was bare-chested, but the woman had wrapped her chest in tight leather straps. Carl couldn't tell if it was out of a sense of practicality or modesty, but it didn't seem to matter much at the time. What was more obvious was the array of scars that covered most of the bare skin they both were displaying, along with the matching Wolfsangel tattoos just below their collarbones.

In any other situation, Carl would've thought it to be too ridiculous to take seriously. They looked like performers in a gothic horror circus, coming to perform a faux-sexual battle dance in an underground Vegas nightclub. Unfortunately, things being as they were, it was obvious they were here to kill him.

Carl and Burgess were on their feet, weapons drawn before the monsters were all the way out of the elevator, the height from their stilts forcing them to duck down and step slowly onto the floor. Carl took a position next to the door of the office, aiming his weapon directly at the woman. Burgess stood in place behind his desk, pointing his gun through his office window at the man.

Get on the ground!" Burgess shouted. "You get one chance!"

His conditions were not accepted. Their wolf jaws opened and they both let out blood-curdling screams as they bolted forward at unreal speeds. The running stilts got them across the office in two very fast steps and Carl fired off two shots out of reflex before he even realized they were on him.

Rather than coming directly at him, as Carl pulled the trigger, the woman sprung to one side, moving instantly out of the line of fire and out of Carl's eyeline. Carl heard a third round go off, and the window to Burgess' office blew out a hole directly in front of where the male wolf had been an instant before.

"They can dodge bullets?!" Carl shouted in disbelief. "These assholes can dodge bullets!"

"Fuck!" Burgess responded, grabbing at the phone on his desk.

Before he could dial, the woman was suddenly in the doorway, her clawed hand swatting the gun out of Carl's hand and drawing a long bloody gash down his arm. An instant later, an office chair came smashing through the office window, hitting Burgess square in the face with metal and glass. The collision sent him reeling backwards, just narrowly missing being sent through the window of his office. Instead, his head and back smacked against the metal frame of the window and he crumpled to the floor, dropping both his gun and the phone as he went down.

The woman swiped at Carl's face with her other claw. He barely managed to dodge the attack, but fell backward onto the floor as he did, frantically looking for his gun.

The male wolf was suddenly in the office with them, jumping gracefully through the window and looking very proud of himself.

Burgess was unconscious on the floor behind the desk, and Carl was starting to panic, not able to locate where either of their guns had fallen.

"Hey, dickface!" a voice shouted from outside of the office.

Both of the wolves turned to look, and Carl followed their gaze. From between the woman's legs he could see out the office door, to Walter standing in the station behind them. In one hand he held what looked like a metal briefcase. In his other hand was some kind of reflective dish, facing outward toward him and the wolves. Upon seeing this, Carl realized he could hear a high-pitched sound that was getting louder and higher pitched very quickly.

"Made you look," Walter said, and there was a popping sound, followed by a bright flash of purple light and the sound of glass exploding.

Carl was instantly blind. The building panic came to a peak as he pounded his hands frantically around the ground, still desperately trying to find either of the guns that were somewhere on the floor. The furious screaming coming from the wolves weren't helping, until it slowly dawned on Carl that it was because they were blind too.

There were two successive crashing sounds that Carl couldn't quite identify, and the screams died down.

"Get up, Carl," he heard Walter's voice say. "We got to go."

"I can't see," Carl said.

"Your legs still work," Walter said. "Just take a deep breath and get up. I can lead you, but I have to carry your friend. He's out cold."

Carl took a deep breath and felt the panic subside.

"I need my gun," Carl said, rolling over to his side to push himself to his feet.

"Goddammit," Walter mumbled. There was a shuffling sound and Carl suddenly felt the butt of his gun pressed into his hand.

"Safety's on," Walter said. "Now let's move. They're not alone."

Carl could hear Walter grunt as he lifted Burgess. A moment later, Walter grabbed Carl's hand and placed it on his shoulder.

"What did you do to me?" Carl asked, holding tight to Walter's shoulder as they made their way to the elevator.

"Just a bright light," Walter said. "You'll be fine in a few minutes."

"What about them?" Carl asked.

"Same thing," Walter said. The change in acoustics told Carl they'd made it into the elevator. "Then I hit 'em with a chair. It was fun."

"You said there are more?" Carl asked, the elevator starting the trip to the ground floor.

"They went to the morgue," Walter said. "Don't worry, there's nobody down there. They just went to get Tyler's body."

"Tyler?" Carl asked.

"The body from the forest," Walter said. "His name is Tyler Sykes. He's a sagittarius."

"You've known who he was this whole time?" Carl said, angrily.

"You were supposed to figure that out on your own," Walter said. "It needed to be done through proper channels. But I guess that's a moot point now."

The elevator stopped and they started moving again. In a few steps, Carl felt the cold air of the outdoors.

"So how did you know?" Carl asked as they stumbled down the sidewalk.

"You wouldn't believe me if I told you," Walter said.

"Try me," Carl pressed.

"No," Walter said, then shouted "Open the door!"

Carl heard the sound of a large van door sliding open a few paces ahead of them.

"You look like you've got this handled," a male voice said, sardonically.

"Shut up and help me," Walter said. "We've got to get this guy to the hospital."

"Step back a second, G-Man," the second voice said, putting a hand on Carl's shoulder and detaching him from Walter.

"Isaac?" Carl blurted, suddenly recognizing the voice. "You're the other boyfriend?"

"I prefer 'boyfriend also,' if you don't mind," Isaac said. "Just stand here a sec. I need to make sure my brother doesn't break your friend's neck."

"Ha ha," Walter said. "Hurry up, he's heavy."

There were more shuffling and grunting sounds as Walter

and Isaac tried to load Burgess into the van without doing any further damage to him.

"Okay, your turn," Isaac's voice said after a moment, and Carl was led into the van.

Carl's vision was already starting to come back. He could make out slight indications of street lights, but not enough to really figure out what was going on. It was still a relief to see any improvement. He could tell that the van didn't have any seats, and he was on the floor with Burgess sprawled out next to him.

The doors of the van slammed shut and the motor started. As they started moving down the streets, Carl gave himself permission to breathe deep and really take in what was happening around him.

"What the fuck just happened?" Carl finally said.

"Neo-Nazi Werewolves just tried to kill you," Isaac said from the driver's seat. "You must be doing something right."

"I got to hit Nazis with a chair," Walter said. "Best day ever."

CHAPTER SEVEN
THE OUTSIDE WORLD

"You guys don't live here, do you?" Carl asked, taking in the surroundings. After leaving Burgess at a hospital, Carl's vision had come back just in time for him to see them pull up to an empty building in the middle of downtown.

The building, on its face, seemed like a prime piece of real estate. Only a few blocks from the riverside, and nestled right between major business blocks and an intersection of some major mass transit lines. Yet, for some reason, a security fence was erected around the building and a "Property For Sale" sign over the main entrance looked like it had faded from years of sun and rain.

Isaac led them to a section of fence that detached with little effort and the three of them entered the building without even looking like they were trying to hide it. Inside, a security guard nodded at them as they made their way to the third floor. This may have been part of why the building wasn't selling; it was only three stories high on a block that seemed to have a ten story minimum.

"Temporary base of operations," Isaac replied, collecting together some of the derelict office furniture for them to sit comfortably in the otherwise wide open floor. "The security guard owes us a favor."

"What kind of favor?" Carl asked.

"A perfectly legal one," Walter said, taking a seat next to one of the floor-to-ceiling windows that overlooked the street.

"His former employer was cutting corners on safety regulations," Isaac said. "We gave him a heads up. Saved his co-workers' lives, and gave him grounds for a lawsuit. The settlement is paying for his daughter's college. So, as long as we're not cooking meth up here, he lets us hang out when we need to lay low."

"Isaac," Walter growled. "You're talking too much."

"Heather said we could trust him," Issac said.

"He's a Fed," Osric said. "Feds don't like people like us."

"What exactly are 'people like us,' Walter?" Carl asked.

"Walter?" Isaac said, smirking. "You told him your name was 'Walter?'"

"I'm not telling him my real name," the grumpy-faced guy said.

"Yeah, but 'Walter?'" Isaac said. "If we're doing fake names, why not cool ones? Like, 'Maverick' or 'Cobra?'"

"Both of those names are stupid," Not-Walter said.

"So, what is his name then?" Carl asked. It was already clear to him that if he didn't say anything, the two of them would probably never stop arguing.

"Don't say it," the fake Walter said, glaring at Isaac.

Isaac appeared to be genuinely torn, glancing back and forth between the scowling face and Carl.

"Osric," Isaac said. "His name is Osric."

"Goddammit, Isaac," Osric said, turning away from them in frustration.

"Issac and Osric?" Carl said. "So, you two really are brothers?"

"Half-brothers," Isaac said. "Our moms didn't know about each other until way later. I think our dad wanted names that sounded the same so if he got us mixed up he could pretend he was misheard."

"Sounds like a real piece of work," Carl said.

"Oh, you don't know the half of it, G-Man," Isaac said.

"That's enough, Isaac," Osric said from his perch by the window.

"Right," Isaac said. "Osric doesn't like talking about the old man. Sets off his anger issues."

Carl made a mental note to delve into that subject later. Of all the bizarre things that he'd come across, not just in this case but in Landfall itself, he had not expected his car-smashing stalker to be so mundane as to just have Daddy Issues.

"Well, how about you tell me about your involvement in my case instead?" Carl said.

"That's a long story," Isaac said. "And, honestly, you don't seem like someone who would handle the news very well."

"That is not for you to decide," Carl pressed. "I am a federal officer, and what you two are doing right now is just shy of kidnapping. So you need to tell me what's going on right now."

"We have to wait for Heather first," Osric replied.

"Is that the girl that was on the phone?" Carl asked. "Is she the one in charge here?"

"Nobody is really in charge," Isaac said. "We're a team.

But, for all intents and purposes, yeah, she's in charge."

"That makes him the muscle," Carl said, tilting his head toward Osric. "And you're, what? The guy who runs around the country collecting old phones?"

"I work at a hotel, Carl," Isaac said, smirking. "The world comes to me."

There was a chiming noise from Osric, who pulled a cell phone from his pocket and checked it.

"She can't get here for another hour," Osric said, grimly.

"Is she okay?" Isaac asked, his voice going soft with genuine concern.

"She said the muffins aren't out of the oven yet," Osric replied.

"She's baking?" Isaac said, grimly. "Maybe one of us should--"

"No," Osric said, shaking his head. "She just says to start without her,"

"Start with what?" Isaac asked, his back suddenly straightening with anxiety.

Osric sighed, not approving of what he was about to say.

"Tell him everything," he said.

"Oh boy," Isaac breathed, turning to Carl. "Big day for you."

"What's going on?" Carl asked, cautiously.

"Just what you wanted," Isaac said, standing and making his way to a single desk against the far wall. "No more Cloak-and-Dagger shit. I'm going to answer all of your questions, and probably change your life in the process."

Isaac took hold of the desk and pulled it across the empty floor to where Carl was sitting, and moved a chair to the other side of it, taking a seat like he was about to interview Carl for a job.

THE OUTSIDE WORLD

"Don't worry, I've got it," Isaac said loudly towards Osric. "I don't need any help or anything."

Osric grunted an almost chuckle and continued watching the street.

"Don't worry," Isaac said to Carl. "I've prepared a small presentation to get you caught up. It should only take about twenty minutes."

"Oh, for fucks sake," Carl said, rolling his eyes.

"Trust me," Isaac said, opening up the desk drawers and looking inside them. "This is the least painful way to get through this."

From inside the desk, Isaac produced a large drawing pad, a set of red, black, and blue felt-tip markers, a bottle of whiskey, and a single drinking glass.

"You're going to need these," Issac said, placing the whiskey and the glass in front of Carl.

After a moment of thought, Isaac took out a second glass and placed it at the far edge of the desk.

"You need some of this, Osric?" Isaac asked. "That cop looked heavy."

"I'm fine," Osric said, not looking away from the window.

"Before I start," Isaac said, "I have a question for you, Carl. What is your relationship with the word 'normal?'"

"I don't follow," Carl said.

"Some people see 'normal' as a dirty word," Isaac said. "In a society that prides itself on its diversity, 'normal' suggests an ideal state of conformity. An elitist mindset, if you will, suggesting that there are things that aren't 'normal' that should be shunned."

"Some folks prefer the word 'typical,'" Isaac continued, "suggesting that there is no such thing as 'normal,' but only commonalities that are statistically dominant. But, there are folks who take issue with that word, too. Calling something 'typical' suggests that it's to be derided for being predictable."

"Has it been twenty minutes yet?" Carl asked.

From the window, Osric chuckled.

"What I'm getting at here," Isaac explained, "is that I'm going to be speaking in generalities, but only for the sake of illustration. People like you are different from people like me, and I don't really have time for this to devolve into a semantic argument over exactly what people like you are called. So, I'm asking you if you prefer to be called 'normal' or 'typical.' I don't care which, so long as you understand that the label is only for the sake of conversation, and not that I'm making any assumption about your value as a person."

Carl took the bottle of whiskey and poured a shot into the glass. He was full of adrenaline a moment ago, but now he just wanted to take a nap until it was all over.

"'Normal' is fine," Carl said, after gulping down the drink.

Isaac nodded and picked up the black felt-tip pen. Centering the drawing pad between them, he drew a circle in the middle of the page.

"This is your world," Isaac said. "The Normal World."

Isaac leisurely colored in the circle with the pen as he spoke, gradually turning the circle into a big black dot.

"Everything you need is there," he said. "A nice calm lake with clean water. Trees with tasty fruit. Lots of rabbits and squirrels to eat. All your friends, all your family. It's where you were born and you have no reason to even think of leaving. It's perfect for you."

Isaac traded the black pen for the blue pen, and drew a larger circle around the Normal World. He then switched out for the red pen, and started drawing lines inside the larger, blue circle, creating a sense of a giant warning sign.

"This is The Outside World," he said. "It's all the places you've never been, and would never want to go. There's big animals with sharp teeth that like to eat people there. There are raging rivers that people drown in. Big, angry mountains that people freeze to death on or fall from. It's a crazy, scary place that nobody in their right mind would want to go.

"But people do go there," Isaac said, setting the pen down and folding his hands in front of him. "Because not everybody born in the Normal World is normal. These people are called 'Weirdos.' They aren't comfortable with the Normal World, and more often than not, the Normal World isn't comfortable with them. So, they go to the Outside World. They might not belong in the Outside World either, but it makes more sense to them than The Normal World does. And while they're out there, they learn what it is. They find the safe passages in the mountains. They learn to swim in a running river. They find out that the big animals taste even better than squirrels. And sometimes, when we're lucky, they bring all that back into the Normal World."

With that, Isaac picked up the black pen again.

"And, when that happens," he said, coloring in the Outside World, turning the whole picture into one big, black dot, "the Outside World becomes part of the Normal World. Your perfect world gets a little bigger, and your perfect life gets a little better. More land, more water, more food."

Isaac put the black pen down and picked up the blue one again.

"But when that happens," he said, "The Outside World doesn't go away."

With the blue pen again, he drew an even bigger circle

around the big black dot, then taking up the red pen and giving the new Outside World its warning stripes.

"As the Normal World gets bigger, so does the Outside World," Isaac said. "Bigger, weirder, and more dangerous. But the weirdos keep going out there. The Outside World never ends, and the weirdos never quit.

"And so goes the history of human evolution," Isaac said, dropping the pen on the desk with finality. "Weirdos set sail for new lands, discover vaccines, walk on the moon, and invent computers. Generation by generation, all that weird shit becomes so normal that you laugh at your ancestors for ever thinking it was weird in the first place. Fifty years from now, your perfectly normal grandkids will be laughing at you from their house on another planet."

"So what you're trying to tell me," Carl interrupted, "is that you're a bunch of weirdos. I thought you said this was going to be life-changing."

"Yes and no," Isaac said. "Osric and I, we're the third kind of person. For lack of a better word, we're oddballs."

"Are you sure there isn't a better word?" Carl asked.

"If you think of one, let me know," Isaac said. "We aren't exactly weirdos, but we're not exactly normal either. We've got a foot in both worlds, and can speak both languages. If need be, we can even pretend to be one or the other. For a little while, anyway. Our job is to keep the process running. We help the normals understand the weirdos. We bridge the divide and keep them helping each other rather than, for example, setting each other on fire."

"And your girlfriend?" Carl asked.

"She's the weirdo," Isaac confirmed. "Heather lives in the Outside World. We help her survive there."

"What does this have to do with missing babies?" Carl

asked.

"Uh, hello?" Issac said, throwing his hands in the air. "They were kidnapped by Nazi Werewolves! How is that not the weirdest shit you've ever heard?"

"And you just decided to make it your business," Carl said. "Interference with an official investigation be damned?"

"As the saying goes," Isaac said, "'When the going gets weird, the weird turn pro.' Ghost stories, alien abductions, urban legends; that's our jurisdiction. If anything, you were interfering with *our* investigation."

"None of those things are real," Carl said.

"Maybe, maybe not," Isaac said. "But plenty of people believe they are. And when they need help, the Normals are nowhere to be found. We help people with weird problems. And this one was a big one. That's why we decided to work with you. We realized we couldn't do this without at least one Normal person to help us."

"Goddamnit," Carl said. "This is just more Landfall bullshit. You haven't answered a single fucking question."

"Maybe you haven't asked the right ones yet," Isaac said.

"Fuck you," Carl shouted to the ceiling. "You said no more games!"

"Fine, fine," Isaac said, waving his hands apologetically. "I'm sorry. Ask your questions. I promise I will answer them plainly and succinctly."

"How the fuck did you know the babies were kidnapped?" Carl said directly.

"Heather is psychic," Isaac said. "When someone needs help, she sees it in a dream. That's how we knew about the babies, the Nazis, and you. Because Heather saw it all in a dream."

Carl looked over at Osric. Osric took a moment to turn

away from the window to return a look to Carl, nodding in confirmation.

"Un-fucking-believable," Carl said.

"Just take a moment to think it over," Isaac said.

"This fucking town," Carl said, exasperated.

"If you just step back and look at the whole picture," Isaac said, "it'll all make sense."

"This makes sense to you?" Carl shouted.

"Think about it," Isaac pressed. "We gave you the exact location of Tyler's body. We even know his name. His real name. Even his Nazi friends don't know that."

"Oh, that's another good question," Carl said. "How the hell was that body supposed to help me with my case?"

"He's one of the victims," Isaac said. "So were the two that attacked you at the station."

"What?" Carl blinked.

"They were all conceived under a full moon," Isaac said. "We only exposed the most recent kidnappings, but this has been going on for almost twenty years."

Carl slumped back in his chair, stunned.

"You were supposed to identify the body as Tyler Sykes," Isaac said. "And then you were supposed to find his family, and the kid they'd been raising as Tyler for the last fourteen years. That was how you connect the Wolfsangel tattoo to the missing kids."

"Well, that didn't fuckin' work, did it?" Carl said, his mind reeling.

"No, that kinda went sideways," Isaac said. "Looks like you just spooked them enough to make them try and kill you. Which kind of counts as a break in the case, right?"

"My partner is in the hospital," Carl said. "And you still haven't given me anything I can use. Like proof of how they swapped out the babies and where they're keeping them. I seriously don't need anything more than that."

"Yeah," Isaac said, looking downward. "We've hit a bit of a wall ourselves."

"What do you mean?" Carl asked.

Isaac shifted nervously in his seat and looked to Osric.

"She said to tell him everything," Osric said, over his shoulder.

Isaac sighed. "We've only been doing this for a couple of years," Isaac said. "This is our first...murder. Heather didn't just see where he was buried, she saw his whole life. And then she saw him die. It fucked her up pretty bad. She hasn't slept since."

"That was two days ago," Carl said.

Isaac nodded. "She's baking," he said. "It's bad."

"How did he die?" Carl asked.

"They make the kids fight," Isaac said. "They strap those claws and masks on them and throw them in a pit to duke it out. Win or lose, they don't give them medical attention until they get themselves out of the fight pit. If you aren't strong enough to get out on your own, then you're too weak to live. He died scared, alone, and in pain, surrounded by people he thought was his family calling him trash."

"Jesus," Carl said.

"Yeah," Isaac said. "I don't think I've ever seen Heather cry so much."

"Why do they do it?" Carl whispered. "It doesn't make sense."

"You ever hear those stories?" Isaac said, "About people who get hypnotized into thinking they can do things they can't, and then they can? They can lift cars and play piano out of nowhere, just because they got totally convinced that they could."

"Those are just urban myths," Carl said.

"I know," Isaac said, "but I think that's what they're doing. I think they're raising these kids to think they're actually werewolves so they'll be more brutal. Maybe they think it actually makes them stronger too, like the hypnosis myths."

"You think they're trying to build an army," Carl said, the horror of it dawning on him. The history of what the Nazis did to their own soldiers with brainwashing and amphetamines were already legendary examples of human monstrosities. To think that they'd actually started doing it to children seemed beyond thinkable. But then again, outdoing themselves on being the worst of the worst had always been their calling card.

"Yeah, I do," Isaac said. "And most of them are teenagers already. The ones that survived, anyway."

"Jesus Christ," Carl whispered. He grabbed at the bottle of whiskey and shakily poured himself a double. "And you got all of this from your girlfriend's dreams, is that what you're saying?"

"Not all of it," Isaac said. "My brother and I do a lot of the legwork, but Heather always points us in the right direction."

"Well, which is it then?" Carl asked. "She can predict which cab I'm going to randomly get into, but she can't tell me how a half-dozen babies got stolen?"

"Actually, the cab was me," Isaac said.

"Are you psychic too?" Carl asked.

"No, I've just lived in Landfall my whole life," Isaac said. "There's only two flights from D.C. a day, and the other one lands in the middle of the night. And the city keeps a pretty tight leash on the cab companies to keep them from fighting over fares in the airport driveway. So, it's a pretty high chance that any cabs that were waiting for fares when the D.C. flight arrives will probably be there at the same time a few days in a row."

"There were six cabs waiting when I left the airport," Carl said. "How did you know which one I'd get into?"

"I didn't," Isaac said. "We gave the number to ten cab drivers."

"Did you pay them all the same twenty bucks?" Carl asked.

"It was only a week's worth of tips," Isaac said, shrugging. "Heather said you needed our help."

"You're bullshitting me," Carl said.

"I couldn't bullshit you if I wanted to, Carl," Isaac said. "I can't lie."

"Oh, really?" Carl asked. "Why's that?" He'd lost count of the number of suspects that had tried to convince him that they were incapable of lying. He couldn't wait to hear what this weirdo was going to say.

"The same reason why alcoholics can't drink," Isaac said.

Carl had to admit, he hadn't heard that one before.

"You said earlier that you're able to pass for normal," Carl said. "When exactly do you plan on doing that?"

"I had you fooled back at the hotel, didn't I?" Isaac said.

"You did not," Carl replied. "So what's your plan now? Now that you've thrown a hornet's nest at me, what's your next big idea?"

"That's what we're waiting for right now," Isaac said. "Once Heather gets here, we'll figure out the next move."

"I can't wait," Carl said, taking hold of the bottle and pouring himself another drink.

* * *

"You called me 'Deep State,'" Carl said, stepping up to the window next to Osric.

"That's what they call you, right?" Osric said, nodding.

"Back at The Bureau, yeah," Carl said. "Before they booted me off the White Power desk. Where did you hear it?"

"When Heather saw you coming to town, I looked you up," Osric said. "An article on some militia you broke up about eight years ago mentioned your nickname. That's how I knew I would like you."

"You like me?" Carl asked, genuinely surprised.

"Of course," Osric said. "Most Normal people just want to live their normal lives without any trouble. You actually want to make the Normal world better. It's admirable."

"Then what's with the dirty looks?" Carl asked.

"What?" Osric said, turning a quizzical look to Carl.

"When you were following me around town," Carl said. "Every time I saw you, you looked like you wanted to choke me out."

"Oh," Osric said. "That's just my face."

"Bummer," Carl said.

"I do okay," Osric replied.

"So, I have a question," Carl said.

"Apparently," Osric said, "I'm supposed to tell you everything."

"Tell me about the Sokolov Brothers," Carl said.

Osric grunted with disapproval. "Those pricks," he said. "Cops were watching them, so they were getting ready to pin everything on their youngest brother and make him take the fall. We got him to Canada before they got the chance."

"That's it?" Carl asked.

"That's the long and short of it," Osric said.

"What about the part where you paralyzed them?" Carl asked.

"Oh, that," Osric said. It sounded to Carl like he'd actually forgotten about it.

"Yeah," Carl said. "That."

"I got careless," Osric said. "They recognized me somehow. It was self-defense."

"You ran them into traffic," Carl said, "in self-defense?"

"That's my story," Osric said.

"How did *you* walk away from that?" Carl pressed.

"I assume your training included hand-to-hand combat?" Osric asked.

"Yeah," Carl said, cautiously.

"And, in the event that you're unable to avoid being hit," Osric explained, "they teach you how to move in a way that minimizes the impact of the hit, correct?"

"You're talking about rolling with the punch," Carl said. "You're saying you rolled with the punch of a car?"

"That's correct," Osric said.

"That's impossible," Carl said.

"Not if you practice," Osric said, matter of factly.

"I need another drink," Carl said, turning back to the desk.

Isaac sat there quietly, studiously reading something on his phone as Carl poured another double into his glass.

Carl was about to gulp the drink down when he stopped and turned to Isaac.

"What about the taser trick?" Carl asked. "Did he practice that too?"

"Every day for a month," Isaac said, not looking up from his phone. "It was my birthday present."

Carl poured another double into the glass before gulping the whole glass down in one go.

Carl steadied himself as the whiskey burned its way down his gut, and he tried desperately to wrap his head around all of it. There was no part of this that wasn't completely insane, but it made more sense for it all to be true than not. Welcome to Landfall.

A shuffling noise from the far corner snapped him out of it. He looked to see a small and exhausted looking girl staggering onto the floor from the stairway. Her dark skin hid most of her features in the shadows, but even from there Carl could see she was barely standing upright as her bloodshot eyes stared out from the dark.

"Did we win yet?" her voice squeaked.

"Jesus, Heather," Isaac said, bolting to his feet as he and Osric rushed to her side.

"You didn't walk here, did you?" Osric asked as they both held on to her to steady her.

"No, no," she said, "I took a cab. He was very nice. He didn't even charge me for the ride. Or, I forgot to pay him. I hope it was the first one."

As they led her into the main area they'd been occupying, Carl could see more clearly now that she had not even bothered to get dressed. She was wearing a bright pink bathrobe over flannel pajamas covered in cartoon unicorns. Her bare feet plod along the dirty carpet as her curly hair swung lazily around her face.

"You need to sleep," Isaac said. "You're a mess."

Her face twisted momentarily in a mix of pain and disgust. "I tried," she said, barely above a whisper. "I really tried."

As she stepped further into the light, Carl got a better look at her. She was barely an adult herself, in her early twenties at most. She, like her cohorts, had a nonspecific look to her. Not thin, but also not large. The only thing about her that could set her apart from a crowd was the huge mane of curly, dark hair that exploded around her head. As she got closer, Carl could see that she hadn't bothered to wash the makeup off her face that had been smeared and streaked from who-knows-how-many hours of crying.

"Nice to finally meet you, Carl," She said, trying to force a smile. "Welcome to the team."

"I am not on your team just yet," Carl said. "I'm still not convinced I shouldn't just haul all of you in."

"I appreciate you giving us a chance," Heather said, saying every word carefully, like she wasn't entirely sure she was saying anything correctly. "Let's have a seat."

She motioned towards the windows and the boys led her over to them, gently setting her on the floor.

"I love the view from here," Heather said as Carl sat on the floor in front of her. "Everything gets that peaceful, faraway look, without being so far away that you feel detached. I feel like Mother Nature watching her little woodland creatures from here."

"Sure, okay," Carl said.

Isaac knelt down next to Heather, holding a glass of whiskey to her.

"I know we've already had this conversation," he said softly to her, "but it's getting really bad, sweetie. If you don't sleep soon, I'm really worried about what will happen to you. Could you please give this a try?"

Heather looked down at the glass, her face twitching in

disapproval. But she eventually nodded and took the glass from him. Taking a sip from it took real effort, as she seemed truly disgusted by the idea of tasting the stuff.

"Have my boys been polite to you?" she asked, once she'd stopped gagging. "I know they can be a handful sometimes."

"They've been the bare minimum of helpful," Carl said.

"I saved your life," Osric said.

"That is the bare minimum," Carl replied.

"I'm already feeling better," Heather said, looking down at the glass. "Maybe this stuff isn't so bad."

She tried to take another sip, and looked like she regretted it as she forced herself to swallow.

"Uhg, I need to trust my instincts," she said to herself.

"They tell me that you're psychic," Carl said, deciding to get it over with before she passed out on them.

She nodded. "It started when I was thirteen," she said. "My family still doesn't believe me, but I realized I don't need them to."

"Is that when you moved to 'the Outside World?'" Carl asked.

Heather grinned. "Isaac gave you the speech, huh?" she said, patting Isaac's knee. "He's very poetic."

"So, you're not living out in the forest?" Carl asked.

"No," Heather said. "We share an apartment. I live in the Outside World metaphorically."

"How does it work, then?" Carl asked.

"It comes to me in my dreams," she said. "Someone, somewhere needs my help, and my dreams show them to me. Sometimes I see the past, sometimes it's the future. Sometimes it's literal, sometimes it's metaphorical."

"And this thing you do," Carl asked. "You and your boys

here."

Heather forced another sip of the booze.

"It took me a couple of years," she said, "but I eventually realized what it was I was seeing. Sometimes if I thought hard enough before going to sleep, I could get answers to specific questions. They weren't always very specific answers, but I kept getting better at it. Then I met my boys, and together we've been able to help more people than I ever thought imaginable. Every day they make me more proud."

"You're drunk," Osric said with a smirk.

"But, why now?" Carl asked. "If you've been saving people for years, and they've been taking kids for decades, why are you only just now exposing them?"

"Because we can, now," Heather said. "I don't ever dream about plane crashes or earthquakes, because there's nothing I can do about those. Whatever force in the universe is out there sending me my dreams, it decided that now was when we could actually do something about this."

"With your help," Isaac said.

"Yes," Heather agreed. "With your help, Carl. I dreamt of you coming here after we sent the letters. You were here to help us, but there was someone standing over you."

"You keep mentioning that," Carl said. "What does that mean?"

"Like I said," Heather said, her words starting to slur ever so slightly. "Sometimes the dreams are metaphorical. Someone's standing over you. They're watching everything you do, and not for a good reason. I think, whoever it was, would've made sure you never found anything if we weren't here to point you in the right direction. Possibly to hurt you if that didn't work."

"You think that's who sent the attack dogs?" Carl asked.

"I don't know," she said, closing her eyes and resting her head against the window.

"Oh, that feels nice," she said, the glass starting to slip from her hands.

Isaac caught the glass and gently took it from her. "I think it's starting to work," he said.

A pathetic whine rose up from Heather as she leaned deeper into the window.

"Poor Tyler," she said, her lower lip trembling as she whimpered. "He knew it was coming. He was terrified for months before it finally happened."

Her eyes suddenly flew open and she bolted upright, inhaling deeply as she forced herself awake again. "I can still hear him," she said, fear in her voice.

"Shhh," Isaac said, rubbing her shoulder, trying to calm her. "It's okay, sweetie. We'll find them. They won't hurt anyone after this."

Heather swayed and blinked as she instinctively tried to fight off the delirium of sleep deprivation. Her gaze wandered upward to Osric, who stood over them all, looking like he wished he could punch whatever was keeping her awake.

"Osric, honey," Heather said, her voice waving like someone who wasn't entirely sure where they were. "How was your day?"

"I got to hit Nazis with a chair," Osric said.

"Aww," Heather cooed. "I'm so happy for you."

"Heather," Carl said, placing his own hand carefully on her shoulder.

Her head wobbled as she slowly turned her focus to him. "Agent Carl," she said, as though it was the first time she'd seen him there.

"I can take it from here," Carl said. "You've helped enough."

Slowly, but definitively, Heather nodded her head once. "Cool," she said. And with that, her body went slack. Her eyes dropped closed and her head thunked against the window as she immediately began to snore.

Isaac heaved a sigh of relief as his own body went slack. "Thank god," he said.

Carl rose to his feet and looked at Osric.

"Thank you," Osric said to him.

"You still got my back?" Carl asked.

"That's my job," Osric said.

"Cool," Carl said. "I'm headed back to the station. Those dogs must've left some kind of evidence behind. I need to get to it before anyone else shows up at the station in the morning."

"Sounds like a good place to start," Osric said. "Isaac?"

"I've got her," Isaac said. "We'll stay here until I hear from you."

Carl and Osric both nodded. "Stay out of sight," Carl said, marching towards the stairs. "We still don't know who's standing over me."

CHAPTER EIGHT
SYMPATHETIC PARTIES

It was past 1:00am by the time Carl got back to the station. The hideout was only a few blocks away, but Carl didn't want to take a chance by going straight there. He walked wide around downtown to approach the station from the opposite direction and enter through the garage.

Carl put his hand on his weapon as the elevator doors opened, just in case the Wannabe Werewolves hadn't actually left. The floor was just as empty and partially dark as he'd left it. From that side of the floor, one would almost think that nothing had happened.

As Carl circled around to Burgess' office, the evidence of the attack became readily apparent. Strewn furniture and broken glass, along with the bullet holes on the opposite wall, gave away the store on this one. There was no covering this up, even if he wanted to. He wouldn't have any trouble telling anyone what happened. Burgess would back him up, if he woke up in time. But, explaining how he'd escaped and why he hadn't called in for three hours was going to be difficult without mentioning The Weirdo and her two

Oddballs.

Carl's eyes scanned over the scene as he tried to decide the best course of action. If there really is someone "standing over him," as Heather kept putting it, then keeping this whole insane mess off the books until morning might buy him some very valuable hours to get to the bottom of it all. No matter how it shakes out, once it becomes an official record that he was attacked by Neo-Nazis, he's on the next plane back to D.C. whether the kids are rescued or not. That fact might even mean that the person "standing over him" was his own boss.

Carl shook his head in frustration. The fact that he was even entertaining advice from a self-proclaimed psychic just shows how insane this whole case was. But even if she wasn't really psychic, even if it was just some sort of con, it was a con that had kept his investigation from hitting a wall days ago. She had an inside track of some kind, preternatural or not.

Not that it really mattered. He was attacked by a pair of bullet-dodging teenagers wearing tricked-out werewolf costumes like a couple of comic book villains. Really, all bets were off here.

Carl focused himself and tried to deconstruct the scene. The device that Osric had used to blind them was on the floor in front of the elevator. The desk most directly to the left of the elevator was missing its chair. Osric had set off the device, blinding them all, and immediately dropped it where he stood, grabbing at the chair as he moved and going full bore against the attackers while they were at their most disoriented.

Carl stepped into Burgess' office. The attack was still fresh in his mind, and he could feel his anxiety welling up as his eyes fell on the broken glass and scattered chairs; the ones he and Burgess had been sitting in so calmly, plus the two that had been used as weapons.

The chair that had been thrown through the window was sitting on top of Burgess' desk, where it had settled after colliding with him and sending him into metal of the window frame. The one that Osric had used as a weapon sat on its side on the floor where Osric had dropped it after it had done its job.

Carl tried to imagine how Osric would have attacked. Carl knew how he would have done it, falling back on his training. But trying to imagine the tactics of someone who practices getting hit by cars so he can run an adversary into traffic was difficult to get into the headspace of.

Osric seemed to be the kind of fighter who acted quickly. His attacks would be efficient, calculated. His body frame suggested he had a fair amount of brute strength, but he seemed to prefer keeping that in reserve for defenses.

Carl stepped out of the office again, taking position where Osric had stood when he set off the bright-light device. Taking long paces forward, he traced what he assumed Osric's path would be directly to Burgess' office, stepping just barely to one side to pick up the chair.

No, not pick it up. It happened so fast, Osric would simply have grabbed it by the back as he ran by. Which means he would've begun swinging it upward as he got to the office doorway, and likely struck full force into the female wolf's face as he came through. She likely would have been still facing downward from the shock of the bright flash. The full brunt of the chair would've hit her square in the face and....

Carl looked upward. Sure enough, a spray of blood traced

across the ceiling of the office. Osric had struck her hard enough that her own helmet had broken her nose. Likely knocking her out cold in the process.

From there, it wasn't hard to imagine Osric using the momentum of the chair falling to Earth to simply pull it downward onto the male wolf standing only a few inches to the side. It was unlikely the second attacker was facing upward at that moment, so the second strike probably didn't hit him in the face. The lack of blood anywhere near there seemed to confirm that. But that would mean that Osric had struck him hard enough to knock him unconscious even through the protection of the wolf-shaped helmet. It was already unnerving how much abuse Osric seemed to be able to withstand. If he was equally as capable of dishing it out, that would make him more than just a line of defense for Heather. He'd be a dangerous weapon as well.

The more important question at hand; did the werewolves leave on their own two feet, or were they dragged out by accomplices? Isaac's account of how Tyler died suggested that they were in the habit of leaving the injured to fend for themselves, but the rules may be different where a body might be discovered by the authorities. They had definitely gone through enough trouble just to recover Tyler's body and take him and Burgess out of the equation.

Carl found a possible answer when he turned to see a bloody handprint smearing the inside of the door frame. Had the girl woken up and walked out on her own? If she was carrying the boy as she did, she still had one hand free to steady herself. Meaning, if they left together, he was at least mostly on his feet as well.

It was also possible that the handprint belonged to Osric. Carl was too blind to see if any blood had gotten on Osric when they were hauled out of the station, and if there was, it could just as easily belong to Burgess as much as the two attackers.

So perhaps one, if not both of his attackers were still out there, but suffering from serious head injuries.

Carl looked up at the blood splatter on the ceiling. There was little doubt that it belonged to the female attacker. Would it be worth taking a sample? If these Nazi Werewolf Soldiers were kept off the grid since birth, there wouldn't be any DNA records to compare it to, just like with Tyler.

On the other hand, these two felt seasoned. The attack didn't feel like a couple of kids out on their first assignment. Something about the assuredness they'd moved with gave Carl the feeling that they had done this before.

They dodged bullets. Carl had seen a lot of things in his years at The Bureau, but he'd never seen that before. That was not something people just do.

Maybe this wasn't their first hunt. Maybe a DNA sample wouldn't give them an ID, but it might give them a history. What are the chances that the girl's blood matches up with any open cases?

Carl pulled open the drawers of Burgess' desk and found a swab kit. Looking up at the ceiling, he took a moment to consider the integrity of the crime scene. The most ardent, law-abiding angel on his shoulder told him that standing on Burgess' desk to take the sample would cast doubt on the chain of custody in a court of law, and that he should wait for a lab tech to do it properly. The angry devil of justice on his other shoulder just kept screaming "Fuck the Nazis" without offering any real counterplan.

Carl decided to compromise by carefully kicking his shoes off before stepping up onto the desk. If a lab tech were there, they might say that stepping onto the desk with sweaty socks would contaminate the crime scene just as much, if not more, than dirty shoes. But, in the moment, Carl felt that the spirit of the gesture was what was important.

Reaching carefully up to the ceiling, Carl swabbed at the blood splatter and sealed it away into the sample container.

Now what? Carl asked himself, peering at the sample container. He'd sent hundreds of DNA samples to the lab for testing, but never before had he needed to know what happened to them when they got there.

"This doesn't look good," a voice said.

Carl's attention snapped to the door of the office, where a uniformed officer stood, scowling at him.

"FBI," Carl said, reflexively as he climbed down off the desk.

"I know who you are, Agent Abrams," the uniformed officer said. "Or would you prefer I call you, 'Deep State?'"

Something in the way he said that made Carl feel that he didn't mean it as a compliment. Carl looked over the officer as he slipped his shoes back on. The officer was an older, heavier gentleman who looked like he'd been stuck behind a desk for the last twenty years and was still bitter about it.

"Agent Abrams is fine," Carl said. "You on duty right now?"

"Just on my lunch break," the uni said. "But I think I should be asking you what you're doing here, in the middle of the night, fiddling about with what looks like a crime scene inside my station."

"It's complicated," Carl said. "Lieutenant Burgess and I were attacked earlier. I needed to collect evidence."

"You couldn't wait for the lab techs to do that for you?" the officer asked, not scowling any less.

"Look," Carl said, "Officer…?"

"Banks," the officer said. "Stuart Banks. I'm the Sergeant on duty. If there was an attack here tonight, why am I learning about it just now?"

"Still complicated," Carl said. "I'm going to need you to trust me."

"I have absolutely no reason to trust you," Sergeant Banks said, gently placing a hand on his gun. It didn't worry Carl, at first. The way the weapon rested on Banks' hip suggested he'd gained almost thirty pounds since the last time he'd needed to draw it from that holster. It would take him forever to try it now.

Before Carl could think of what to say to soothe the Sergeant's mind, Carl's eyes fell on one of the desks in the main office, just behind Banks. Sitting on the desk was a utility tub filled with cleaning supplies. It looked like anything a cleaning crew might use for basic tidying up, but the office cleaning crew had left for the night even before the attack, and Carl was more than sure that this particular tub of cleaning supplies had not been there when he entered the office.

"Come up here on your lunch break every night?" Carl asked.

"What's it to you?" the Sergeant retorted.

"I'm just curious if patrolling the floors is part of your usual routine?" Carl said. "Maybe you saw something that could help us identify our attackers."

"Sorry to disappoint," Banks said. "I got an agreement with some of the guys on this floor. If I'm short on change for the vending machine, they've given me the okay to raid any leftovers in the fridge. I've only just come up here now."

"Uh huh," Carl said, slipping the DNA sample into his

pocket. "And where have you been all night?"

"Excuse me?" Banks snorted. "The fuck you trying to say?"

"If you've been on duty all night," Carl said, "How come you didn't notice someone came here to kill us?"

Banks didn't respond right away. His breathing seemed to get more labored as he stared down Carl. Though, from the size of him, Carl figured just looking at someone hard enough was plenty to make him short of breath.

"Looks like we're at an impasse," Banks said finally. "If you can see past me dropping the ball, then I can look past you tampering with a crime scene before calling it in."

Carl thought it over. It didn't look too good for Sergeant Banks, but Carl wasn't ready to jump on it yet. If he was wrong, he could say goodbye to any police support until Burgess was out of the hospital.

"Look," Carl said, pulling the DNA sample back out of his coat. "I need to see if I can get a hit on this blood sample. Can you show me where your lab is? After that, I was never here and you can be just as surprised by all this as everyone else in the morning."

Banks made a sucking sound through his teeth, like he was thinking about it but also wanted Carl to know that he didn't want to be thinking about it.

"Alright," Banks said, finally. "Follow me."

Banks said, "follow me," but instead of leading the way, he stepped aside from the door and motioned for Carl to go ahead of him. Carl couldn't read too much into that, since it was a classic Law Enforcement move to make sure you never took your eyes off a suspect. Carl tried to get past him as casually as possible.

Once Carl got into the open space of the main office

area, only two steps from Banks, he stopped and turned.

"One question," Carl said, "do you have any tattoos?"

"What's it to you?" Banks snorted.

"Well," Carl said, "It's just that Burgess told me that you guys contract out all of your blood testing. So, before I let you lead me down some dark hallway with no lab and no cameras, I'd like to make sure you're not a Nazi."

Carl was right; it took Banks far too long to successfully pull his weapon. It gave Carl more than enough time to move forward and knee him in the groin. Banks hit the ground with a grunt, and Carl wasted no time taking the gun from his hand.

"You piece of shit kike," Banks growled, still only barely catching his breath.

"For a master race, you guys sure are easy to smack around," Carl said, putting his knee on Banks' back and yanking the handcuffs off his belt.

"You're already dead," Banks said. "They can find you wherever you go. We've trained them to track better than dogs."

"Uh, okay," Carl said. "Is that how they found me at the police station that I've been working at for over a week? You must be so White Proud."

After cuffing his hands, Carl pulled Banks to his feet, which took far more effort than it should have.

"Get it?" Carl said, pushing Banks toward the holding cells. "White Proud? It's a play on White Pride. You get it, right?"

* * *

Carl was beyond his comfort zone at this point. There

were Nazi's out to kill him, he'd abandoned a crime scene, didn't call it in, returned to tamper with it, then abandoned it again, after throwing a cop into a holding cell and stealing his car keys. Sure, the cop was a Nazi that was coming to hose the crime scene down with bleach and probably would have made a second attempt at killing him. But, Carl wasn't calling that one in either, so out of everything else he'd done that would get him fired, that one might get him arrested.

Banks wasn't talking. All he would say to Carl were the expected racial epithets between repetitions of the "you're already dead" greatest hits. Normally, Carl would use his usual interrogation techniques to sweat something out of him over six or seven hours, but he didn't have that kind of time. So, he stole Banks' car keys and cell phone and left him in the holding cell with his belt and shoelaces. Hopefully he'll get the hint.

Exiting the elevator into the parking garage, Carl looked around for any signs of other officers or even a werewolf or two. The echos of his footsteps confirmed that he was there alone. He knew that Landfall was a small town, and whatever officers they had on duty at night were probably all out on patrol, but it felt a little irresponsible to leave your entire headquarters empty save for one Undercover Nazi.

Carl pressed the fob on Banks' keychain and listened for the sound of automatic locks beeping into place. Once in the car, Carl began scanning through the built-in GPS for the vehicle. There weren't very many destinations that Banks had needed to search for, but that didn't stop that model of car from tracking everywhere he went all the time. A little law-enforcement-know-how was all Carl needed to see where Banks was spending his off time.

The first two addresses were easy enough; the HQ and

his home. Three more locations kept repeating themselves and Carl had to look them up on his own phone to learn what lived at those locations.

The first was a quintessential coffee and donut shop that seemed to be spending way more money than it needed to look quintessential, the second was one of the three take-out places in Chinatown that Burgess had mentioned, and the third looked like a nondescript building. Based on its basic shape and location, it was probably built to be a dorm for a fraternity sometime back in the early 1900's, compact stone columns and all, but that meant it could be almost anything now. The photos Carl found didn't show any signage to suggest it had become a place of business or apartments. It just seemed to sit there, looking old.

"As good a place as any," Carl said to himself, and jammed the keys into the ignition.

Carl was four blocks away from the station, sitting at a red light, when it all came crashing down on him.

What the fuck am I doing? His brain said way too loudly. He'd just, essentially, kidnapped a cop, and now he was about to storm a building that was presumably full of Nazis that think they're werewolves with no evidence other than that's where the cop he kidnapped seems to hang out.

Carl pulled the car over, turned off the ignition, and had a panic attack.

Carl was all too familiar with panic attacks. He'd had them regularly in college, but years of therapy had gotten them under control just in time for him to apply to The Bureau. He still remembered the methods he'd learned to help him get through it, but there was a part of him that almost wanted to lean into the panic. After all, it seemed like panicking was a perfectly normal reaction to the situation.

He didn't have the backing of The Bureau or the local police, and the clock was ticking on when they would both be gunning for him. His only hope was a trio of authentic Landfall wackos, and even if he was right about everything, he would likely end up brutally dead. All things considered, it's a wonder he hadn't started panicking sooner.

Once the panic subsided, Carl checked the time. This one had lasted fifteen minutes, a personal record. More importantly, it was almost Two in the morning now, and he still didn't have a plan. In three hours, the first round of Day Shift officers would start arriving at the HQ, and all Hell would break loose.

The high-pitched tones of "Born In The USA" suddenly cut through Carl's thoughts, making him jump in his seat as he groped for the burner phone.

"You still with us, Carl?" Osric's voice said, not even a hint of concern in his voice.

"Where have you been?" Carl asked.

"I was parked outside the station," Osric said. "Now I'm parked a block behind you. You looked like you were having a moment."

"Yeah, you could say that," Carl said. "The good news is, the wolves didn't kill anybody to get into the station. Bad news is, it's because the Night Sergeant is on their side."

"Fuck," Osric said. "What happened?"

"Not a lot," Carl said. "He's in a holding cell for now. But if the rest of the department shows up before I have any hard evidence…"

"Yeah, I get it," Osric said. "How much time do we have?"

"Maybe a couple of hours," Carl said. "I've got a location, but no backup, and I've got evidence, but no way to process it."

"What's the evidence?" Osric asked.

"The girl you clocked in the face," Carl said. "Her blood was still there. I got there just in time before the accomplice poured bleach on it. But there's no lab at the HQ. They hire an outside lab, and I have no idea who that is."

"If Tyler's blood got you nowhere," Osric asked, "how will this blood do anything?"

"I've got a feeling this wasn't the first night out for those two," Carl said. "If there's any open cases that they've bled on before....it's a long shot, but it's all I've got."

"If it works?" Osric asked.

"If it works," Carl said, "I can punch down their door with the entire police force and the Girls Scouts to back me up."

"And if it doesn't?" Osric asked.

"Then I have to go in there alone," Carl said. "And hope that the babies are actually in that building, otherwise I'm probably going to jail. Assuming they let me leave alive."

Carl thought about it for a moment.

"Actually," he said, "there's probably no way to avoid going to jail at this point. I've really gone off the rails here."

"I'm texting you an address," Osric said. "Take the sample there. Tell them you're a friend of Heather's. They'll take it from there."

The phone buzzed at the receipt of a text.

"What are you going to do?" Carl asked.

"I'll watch your location," Osric said. "Send me the address, and I'll keep an eye on it. If I see anything that could be considered 'probable cause,' I'll call you."

"You sure you want to get that close without backup?" Carl asked.

"Hopefully, they still don't know I exist," Osric said. "We don't have a choice. You need to get that sample processed. Get moving."

The line went dead; Osric's signature move for ending a conversation.

Carl typed in the address of the stone building to Osric, then loaded the address he'd received from Osric into the GPS. The address belonged to a house on the other side of the river. As Carl turned the car around, he could feel another panic attack starting to set in, but this time he managed to keep it under control.

Now was not the time to panic.

CHAPTER NINE
BLOOD IN THE WIRES

Twenty minutes later, Carl was pulling up to a run-down single-level house sandwiched in between a lovely residential zone and the freeway. It looked like the kind of place that should have been bulldozed when the neighborhood was gentrified, but the little old lady who lived there refused to die.

Carl parked the stolen car on the other side of the street, three houses down from his destination. He didn't want to take the chance that anyone would come looking for it or later want to check where it's been, be they law enforcement or Werewolf.

The automatic safety lights clicked on as Carl marched up the walk. It gave him something of a comfort to know that if anyone saw him approaching the house at that hour, nobody could accuse him of sneaking up on the place.

Carl knocked as loudly as he could, hoping against hope that whoever he was supposed to meet here was some hopeless insomniac that would be awake anyway.

The door popped open, stopped in its tracks by a security

chain. The face on the other side of the chain wasn't that of a little old lady. It wasn't even a face at all. The face of the woman was noticeably higher. Carl estimated her at six-and-a-half feet tall. It was unlikely she was wearing heels at this hour, but a man could only hope.

"Can I help you," she said with a voice that was almost comically mismatched to her stature. If Carl had heard her voice before seeing her, he would have assumed she was a small child.

"Special Agent Carl Abrams," Carl said, lifting his badge up high for her to see it. It was the first thing he'd done within protocol for hours. "I'm a friend of Heather's."

The woman nodded at him and shut the door. The chain behind the door rattled loose before she opened it wide again, standing aside for him to enter.

"Have a seat," she said, motioning toward a sofa in the middle of the main room as she shuffled into the kitchen. "Would you like some coffee?"

"Yes, thank you," Carl said, stepping near the couch, but choosing to remain standing for the time being. "I'm sorry, but they didn't tell me who I'd be meeting here."

"Shannon Larsson, Esquire," she announced from the kitchen. "I'm Heather's attorney. What can I help you with, Agent?"

"You're a lawyer?" Carl said, confused. "I needed a blood sample tested for DNA. They told me to come to you."

"Oh," Shannon said, a hint of relief in her voice. "You want my husband."

She didn't say anything after that. She fell quiet and focused her attention on preparing the coffee maker.

"Is he here?" Carl asked, cautiously.

"Yeah," Shannon said. "Just give him a second."

She spun her finger around the room as if to indicate an all-seeing presence.

"He can hear us," she said. "The whole place is wired."

There was a sound of someone marching up a flight of steps before a door to the side of the kitchen opened up. Out of it stepped a man with bright green hair, barely tall enough to come up to Shannon's bust, and still wearing his sleep mask.

No, not a sleep mask. It was a domino mask; the kind you would see bank robbers or Superman villains wear in old black-and-white movies.

No, he wasn't wearing the mask. It was painted directly onto his face.

No, it wasn't painted on. It was tattooed on. He had an old-timey burglar's mask permanently tattooed onto his face.

Welcome to Landfall.

"Nice to meet you, Agent Abrams," the man said. "I'm Tunder. Come on down."

Carl looked toward Shannon, and she nodded reassuringly at him.

"I'll bring the coffee down when it's ready," she said.

"You both are being remarkably hospitable about all this," Carl said.

"We've been working with Heather for a year now," Shannon said, sleepily. "You wouldn't be here if it wasn't important."

"Presumably this is life or death?" Tunder added. "Ticking clock? Fate of the world?"

"Mostly just the ticking clock," Carl said. "But maybe a smidge of the other two, yeah."

"Better get to it, then," Tunder said, and turned back down the stairs.

131

Carl followed Tunder down the narrow staircase into the basement. The completely finished basement looked more like a standard suburban home than the ground floor did. The walls and carpet were a basic cream color one would expect in any new house that didn't want to stand out too much, and the furniture looked like they'd simply transplanted a showroom display from a department store.

The entire basement footprint matched the main house upstairs, and Tunder took them down a long hallway to what was presumably where the DNA sample needed to go.

"If you don't mind me asking," Carl said, "but what kind of name is 'Tunder?'"

"It's Hungarian," Tunder said. "It's actually pronounced 'Tündér,' but Nana's been dead for years, so whatever."

"And how do you know Heather?" Carl asked.

"That would be privileged information," Tunder replied. "As my wife would say."

They came to a door at the furthest end of a hallway, and Tunder opened it, not even pausing for the dramatic effect that Carl felt should have accompanied it when he saw what was inside.

The room looked like, for lack of any better reference, a Mad Scientist's lair. There were stacks of computers, chemistry sets, tools mounted on walls that looked like they could be used for either woodworking or medical exams, and even a bodyform mannequin with a half-finished white dress on it.

"And what is it you do, Tunder?" Carl asked, hopefully in a non-accusatory tone.

"I write music for commercials," Tunder said. "But I've picked up a few hobbies over the years."

"Like DNA sequencing, I presume," Carl said.

Tunder motioned towards an expensive-looking bit of machinery resting on a desk next to a laptop.

"The future of mankind's evolution will be by intelligent design," he said, sounding like a commercial himself.

"How does one get into the gene-editing hobby?" Carl asked.

"I was trying to make myself taller," Tunder said. "As a wedding gift. But I'm over that now. Funny story; turns out the only reason she dated me in the first place is because she's into shorter guys."

"Communication is important in a relationship," Carl said, desperately hoping that would end the conversation.

"Fuck yeah, it is," Tunder said, pointing a finger at Carl as though he'd made a groundbreaking revelation. "You got the sample?"

Carl dug the swab container out of his pocket and handed it to Tunder.

Tunder broke open the seal and went to work. With the deftness of a professional, he'd smeared the sample on a slide and had it inserted into the expensive-looking machine in under a minute.

"And we're done," Tunder said, as the machine beeped to life. "We should know who this is in about an hour."

Carl blinked. "Wait," he said. "You're not just sequencing it? You can actually run the results against records?"

"Well, I can't," Tunder said. "But there are some guys on the message boards who can. Between them we've got criminal records, unsolved cases, and genealogy."

"I'm not a lawyer," Carl said, "but I don't think that's legal."

"My wife is a lawyer," Tunder said. "and it's not. But I figure if you're here, whatever you're doing probably isn't legal either."

"Not in the strictest sense, no," Carl said.

Shannon entered then, holding three cups of coffee.

"Did we save the world yet?" she asked, handing cups to Carl and Tunder.

"Still processing," Tunder said. "Wanna play 'I Spy?'"

Shannon smirked at him and turned to Carl.

"So," she said, "what has our girl gotten you mixed up in?"

"White supremacists kidnapped a bunch of infants," Carl said. "Looks like they're raising them to believe they're werewolves."

The two of them didn't react at first. They seemed to be waiting for there to be more to the story.

"Why the fuck are they doing that?" Tunder finally said.

Carl shrugged and sipped his coffee. "Nazis gonna nazi, I guess," he said.

"Where'd this blood sample come from?" Shannon asked.

"I was attacked earlier tonight," Carl said. "One of them dropped that. I've got a possible location, but I need something that lets me bust down a door. I get the feeling that just knocking won't go well for me."

"Have you met Osric?" Tunder asked. "You should take Osric with you."

"Here we go," Shannon said, rolling her eyes.

"What?" Tunder said. "It's a valid suggestion."

"He's obsessed with Osric," Shannon said to Carl.

"Why aren't you?" Tunder pleaded to Shannon. And then to Carl, "Have you seen what that freak can do?"

Carl nodded, consciously choosing not to bring up the irony of someone with a mask tattooed on their face calling anyone a freak. "I heard he ran some guys into traffic, sure," he said. "He said he practices rolling with it."

"Oh, sure," Tunder said, dismissively. "Maybe Isaac can't lie, but Osric is completely full of shit. Did he tell you what hit him that day?"

"What do you mean?" Carl asked.

"It was a Mail Truck," Tunder said. "Not just some car. Not some dinky little Volkswagen. It was a fully loaded Mail Truck. He didn't roll with it, he fucking bounced off it. I was there. I saw it. He should be fucking dead."

"Calm down, honey," Shannon said.

"I want to sequence his DNA so fucking bad," Tunder said, rocking back and forth in his seat.

"Is that how you know them?" Carl asked. "Did you stalk him after you saw what he could do?"

Tunder's mouth started to open with an answer, but Shannon cut in.

"You don't have to answer that," she said, in perfect lawyer tone.

Tunder took the hint and snapped his mouth shut.

Mercifully, the expensive-looking machine made a "bing" sound and Tunder immediately turned his attention to the laptop sitting next to it.

"Alright, we've got our results," he said, glancing at the spectrograph that appeared on his screen. "At a glance I can tell you that it's a Caucasian female, but you probably already knew that."

"I'm mainly looking for any possible criminal activity," Carl said. "But, you said something about genealogy?"

"All those people sending in spit to see if they're descended from Genghis Khan," Tunder nodded. "All those results are saved and indexed. I've got a buddy in the wires with access to that. If she's got an uncle or cousin in there, we'll find them."

"That might come in handy too," Carl said. "It's likely she's a kidnapping victim herself."

"Wonderful," Shannon grumbled. "I'm feeling sorry for a Nazi. I already hate today."

"Everybody comes from somewhere, Love," Tunder said, clacking away at the laptop keyboard.

"Sent," he declared a moment later. "Hopefully, we'll have your answers before too long."

Carl checked the time; he had a little over two hours before he lost control of the entire situation.

"I need to go," Carl said. "Can I get you to do me another favor?"

"Only if it'll piss off Nazis," Shannon said.

"Then you're gonna love this," Carl smiled.

* * *

Too many minutes later, Carl was in the stolen car and heading back over the river. Osric would've been at the Suspect Location for over an hour by now, but Carl hadn't received any message from him. If what Tunder was saying was true, there probably wasn't any reason to worry, but Carl wasn't sure Tunder was a totally reliable source. He seemed like the kind of person who was susceptible, if not a slave, to hyperbole.

A single produce delivery truck passing Carl as he rolled over the bridge reminded him that it wasn't just the Morning Shift of police officers he had to worry about, but that the whole city was starting to wake up. That new addition to an already volatile powder keg had an immediate effect on Carl's mind, and he felt the panic start to take hold again.

Keep it together, Carl told himself. He'd worked with enough counselors questioning trauma victims to know how to deal with panic attacks, but it's difficult to remember the coping methods while also driving a car. The curse of a panic attack is that you're not able to focus on anything, and you find yourself not thinking at all, only feeling the overwhelming fear. If, by some miracle, you're able to force a cognizant thought in there, that's usually where you would employ any number of exercises to abate the panic. But, if that small and tenuous slot of rational brainspace is already filled with keeping a car from veering off a bridge, you're basically fucked.

Mercifully, Carl made it over the bridge and managed to pull the car over. The city was still asleep enough that he didn't need to risk full panic looking for a parking spot. Not sure why he felt the need to, perhaps just because he was operating mostly on autopilot, Carl turned the motor off, pulled the keys out of the ignition, and screamed his bloody head off.

It was a mighty, blood-curdling, ear-splitting scream, ending in Carl pushing the last of the air out of his lungs and momentarily choking on his own dried-out throat. He felt himself nearly pass out as he fell into a fit of dry coughs that prevented him from taking a full breath in for several seconds, and even threatened to start a cascade of gagging and vomiting. It was a truly ugly sight.

When it was over, Carl felt better. Calm, awake, and perhaps a little euphoric from the adrenaline rush he'd just forced on himself. More than anything, he was a little bewildered. According to the councilors he'd worked with, that wasn't really supposed to work.

Carl took a moment to dry the tears off his eyes and face

with his coat sleeve before pulling the burner phone from his pocket.

The line rang until Heather's snarky outgoing message played. Carl ended the call and tried again, with the same results. This didn't really add to Carl's anxiety, as much as confirmed it.

With a deep breath, he slid the key back into the ignition and directed the car towards the suspicious building and whatever ridiculous, evil chaos it may be harboring.

CHAPTER TEN
SLEEPING DOGS AND LIES

C arl circled the block, trying to see if there were any signs of anyone actually being inside the building, and also trying to spot where Osric may have parked the van. Neither endeavor was very successful.

Leaving Banks' car on the opposite side of the block, Carl strolled around to the front of the building, staying on the opposite side of the street. He still didn't have his Probable Cause, and didn't want to draw too much attention to himself until he was ready to make his move.

As Carl made his way down the street, peering at the building as he strode with what he hoped was a non-threatening gait, he fingered at both of the phones in his pocket, trying to will one of them to come to life. A call from Osric or a message from Tunder, whichever came first would be all that mattered.

The street remained quiet. No lights were on in the building, no cars or delivery trucks traveled down the street. Carl suddenly stopped his fake-casual walk and stood on the sidewalk, facing the old building across the street. The building stared obliviously back at him, as if to say "nice weather we're having, eh Stranger?"

"Fuck," Carl muttered to himself. "Now what?"

The building answered him, opening its front doors and spitting Isaac out onto the steps.

"Howdy, G-Man," Isaac called to him.

"Isaac?" Carl shouted. "What the fuck are you doing?"

"Oh," Isaac said, looking back at the building, "We totally broke into this place. You should come arrest us, or something."

With that, Isaac promptly disappeared back inside.

Carl wanted to shoot him, so he counted his breaths until the urge passed.

Checking the time, Carl saw he had less than an hour before the next shift started. It was possible, but not likely, that some officers and detectives might already be arriving at HQ and would find Banks in the holding cell any second now. He had no time to lose.

Carl bolted across the street and pushed his way directly into the building. In the building's foyer, Heather stood arm-and-arm between Osric and Isaac, all three of them looking smug.

"Welcome to my party," Heather said, grinning ear to ear. "Did you bring me a present?"

"What are you doing awake already?" Carl asked.

"I know you said you got this," Heather said. "But you don't got this. I saw in a dream that you still need us."

"You dreamt that I needed you to commit Breaking And Entering?" Carl asked.

"No, that was just a fun idea I had," Heather said.

"So why did I just drive to the other side of the river," Carl asked, "on a slim-to-none chance of a blood sample?"

"It never hurts to have a Plan B," Heather replied.

"Was there ever a Plan A?" Carl asked.

"Don't you want to hear what she saw in her dream?" Isaac asked.

"Not even a little," Carl said.

"I knew he'd say that," Heather said, winking to Isaac.

"Why didn't you answer when I called?" Carl asked Osric.

"Sorry," Osric said, "it must've been while we were still underground."

"Underground?" Carl asked.

"Ahem," Isaac coughed.

"You have the floor, Isaac," Heather nodded, and stepped to one side to give him plenty of room.

"You are standing in the secret clubhouse of The Ironwood Sparrows," Isaac said, opening his arms wide like a well-trained tour guide. "A secret society within the University of Landfall. Rumor has it, it's been a hundred years since Landfall had a mayor that wasn't a member of this very exclusive fraternal order."

"I love it when he does this," Heather whispered to Carl.

"As it turns out," Isaac continued pacing around the foyer, motioning his hands in all directions, "The Ironwood Sparrows was actually a collegiate chapter of The Freemasons. Apparently, that little tidbit wasn't divulged to the pledges until their senior year, but everybody who joined this little club went directly to The Freemason Lodge upon graduation.

"But that was a long time ago," Isaac said, stopping his sweeping movements, and settling back into the center of the room. "Freemasons are less of a clandestine society nowadays, so they shut down the secret clubhouse and sold it off. It's been owned by some Italian shell company for the

141

last thirty years.

"But!" Isaac exclaimed, thrusting a finger into the air for emphasis. "It was still active back in the 1910's, when a well-connected developer named Solomon Rutherford Stanton was contracted to build a subterranean tunnel system for the city of Landfall."

"Stanton?" Carl asked. "You mean, like the hotel?"

"Exactly," Isaac said. "Half this city was built by the Stanton family, and young Solomon was the one who convinced the city that it needed a pedestrian subway. I theorized that his plans must've included direct access to his old dorm, probably so he wouldn't have to stop going to the parties after graduation. Mostly based on my personal experience with rich legacy brats like him. And, I was right. Two floors down, we just walked right in."

"You used the tunnels?" Carl asked.

"We used the tunnels," Heather confirmed, clearly very proud of the accomplishment.

"I thought the tunnels were impossible to navigate," Carl asked.

"We have a map," Isaac said. "Duh."

"Everybody has a map," Carl said. "They're supposed to be no good. Every time I step foot in Landfall people fall over themselves to tell me never to go into the tunnels."

"You're an outsider," Osric said. "We were born here."

"Okay," Carl said, "that doesn't make any damn sense, but we don't have time to get into it now. What have you found so far?"

"Nothing," Osric said. "We just got here."

"There's a dining hall below us," Heather said, "and the tunnel entrance is one floor below that. All the other doors were locked. We were about to start kicking them down when we saw you."

"No security," Carl asked. "No even any guards?"

"Nobody's tried to kill us yet," Isaac said, "so I guess not."

"If this place is the Neo-Nazi Werewolf HQ," Carl said, "then why would they leave it wide open like this."

"Good question," Isaac said, "I have two theories. One; these idiots believe in magic. And since this place used to be a secret hideout for Freemasons, they think that it's still protected by Freemason Invisibility spells."

"Freemason Invisibility Spells?" Carl asked.

"Trust me, they have them," Isaac said. "I base that theory off the fact that looking around the framing of this room, they've taken great care in preserving the Freemason symbols that were carved into the building when it was built. It's not like a Nazi to give a shit about Freemason traditions unless they saw them as exploitable."

"What's the second theory," Heather asked.

"That they absolutely have security," Isaac said, "and they're staying out of sight until backup arrives to kill us all. I'm basing that theory off the dog statue behind me with one eye that looks like a tiny camera."

"Jesus, Isaac," Osric growled. "You couldn't have mentioned that earlier?"

"I only just noticed it when I was giving Carl the history lesson," Isaac said.

"Great, awesome, good plan guys," Carl said, looking around the room for ideas.

"In our defense," Heather said, "none of us have gotten much sleep."

"Looks like we're back to Plan A," Isaac said. "Kick in every door."

Osric nodded and did just that. In short, efficient, and swift movements he rounded the entire foyer and kicked every door in before Carl could even take a breath to object.

"Stop," Carl said, as the last of the six doors blew open under Osric's foot. At least now Carl could honestly report to his superiors that he tried to stop him.

"Good hustle there, Carl," Isaac said, as Heather patted Carl's arm pityingly.

"You know I'm going to have to arrest you when this is all over, right?" Carl said to Osric.

"I know you'll have to try," Osric responded, giving no indication if that was a joke or a threat. "I promise I won't hold it against you."

"I call dibs on Hitler's Head!" Isaac shouted, and quickly ran into one of the freshly opened rooms.

"Goddammit," Carl said, and followed him in.

The room appeared to be a standard Secret Society Library. Floor-to-ceiling shelves lined every wall, and glass cases housed very old looking tomes alongside random museum pieces that presumably had a literary and/or racist history.

"Ew," Heather said as she followed Carl into the room.

"Not a fan of libraries?" Carl asked, surprised.

"Not a fan of *this* library," Heather said. "Bad vibes."

"Yeah," Isaac said. "You can practically smell the eugenics references."

Carl looked around the room for anything of significance. As fascinating as all this would be for an anthropologist or criminal profiler, it wasn't what he needed at the moment. He needed some sort of clue as to where the children were being kept, not their homework assignments.

The most notable item in the room was a glass-encased

wolf skull at the center of the far wall, which seemed to be standing guard over a particularly worn book. The book itself would've been almost unnoticeable if not for its guardian. It was leatherbound, but small; closer to the size of a pocket manual than what Carl would consider a proper book.

The etching on the cover looked like English, but wasn't any version of English that Carl could read.

"Can I keep this?" Isaac asked, pointing to the wolf skull.

"No," Carl said, and continued looking for anything that looked like a filing cabinet or Secret Evil Plans Box.

"Aw," Isaac said.

"Where would you even keep it?" Heather asked.

"Above the sofa," Isaac said. "So he can watch TV with us."

"There's nothing here," Carl said. "Nothing we can use, anyway."

"What about this book?" Isaac said, pointing to the book the wolf skull was guarding. "Looks important."

"It probably is important to them," Carl said, turning to leave the room. "Let's move along. We don't know how long we've got until the racist cavalry arrives."

"Isn't that just the cavalry?" Heather said, following him out.

Back in the foyer, Osric was peering out the windows.

"Still no sign of anybody," Osric said. "But they're probably going to sneak up on us anyway."

"Did any of the rooms you kicked in look like an office?" Carl asked.

Osric pointed to a door at the far end of the room, next to the staircase.

Carl nodded and went to the door, Isaac following behind him like an excited puppy.

It was indeed an office. It looked like the office of a Nazi officer in old movies. Swastikas and Red themed interiors in all directions. The only thing missing was a 20's style gramophone playing a tuba-heavy marching band in one corner.

"Okay," Carl said. "Find something."

Carl went for the desk as Isaac began pulling out filing cabinet drawers.

Heather strolled calmly into the office and took in the room.

"Oh, this guy's an asshole," she observed.

"Stop the presses," Isaac retorted.

Carl opened draws full of pens, knives, keys, and bullets before he found one that contained files. He rifled through them, looking for anything that stood out as especially insidious. Most of it seemed to be run-of-the-mill forms for non-profit tax filings and HR complaints.

One of the folders appeared to be filled with receipts and contracts. Carl pulled that file and started flipping through them, looking for anything along the lines of "Kidnappers R' Us."

Isaac dutifully flipped through each filing cabinet, glancing at each tab and and a quick look inside each folder, taking a lay of the land before focusing on any one file.

"These are all people," Isaac said, after going through two of the drawers. "All of the files have a person's name on them. A lot of clusters of the same last name, so probably families. I can't tell if they're members or people they're targeting, or what."

"Probably a little bit of everything," Carl said. "Look if any of the names match our missing kids."

Isaac nodded and turned his attention back to the files.

Heather strode carefully around the room, taking in the paraphernalia that littered the room like a cluttered mind. As she rounded around the walls, a scowl grew deeper into her face, threatening to become permanent.

"That's him," she said suddenly, stopping at a photo that hung on the wall.

Carl and Isaac looked up at her.

"Who?" Carl asked.

"The one standing over you," she said. "He's in this photo."

Carl stepped around the desk to get a closer look.

The photo looked like it should have been a painting; a portrait of seven grown men and one boy. Each of them were dressed in dark, elegant suits and looked as serious as scorned principals at a Catholic school. Behind them was a red and gold tapestry that seemed to have every offensive symbol in every culture woven into it.

"Which one?" Carl asked.

Heather tapped a finger on the photo, directly onto the boy.

"This one," she said. "He's older now, but it's definitely him. He looked just as angry in my dream."

"Who the fuck are these people, then?" Carl asked.

Heather grabbed the photo off the wall and smashed it against the desk, digging the photo out and flipping it over. The back of the photo was blank.

"No idea," Heather said.

"You know," Carl said, "the frame just opens right up on the back."

"That was more fun," Heather smiled.

"Hold up," Isaac interrupted. "I just realized something."

Pulling a handful of the files out, Isaac moved to the desk

and opened them.

"All of these last names are names of the moon," Isaac said.

"What?" Carl asked.

"The old calendars before the Romans took over," Isaac said. "You've heard of Hunter's Moon and Harvest Moon, right? Each full moon of the year has its own name. All these surnames; Strawberry, Buck, Cold, those are all phases of the moon."

"So, these are codenames then?" Carl asked.

"Yeah, but look inside," Isaac said, opening the files up and spreading them around the desk.

"Those are grades," Isaac continued, talking faster as he opened four more files and shuffled them around for Heather and Carl to look them over. "Disciplinary records, medical exams."

"Oh my god," Heather said. "These are the kids. These are the kids they're raising."

"And look at this one," Isaac said, putting an open file in Carl's hands.

At the top of the first page of the file, a single word "FAILED" was rubber-stamped in red.

"Failed?" Carl said. "Oh, shit. This kid is dead."

"They kept all the files on all the kids," Isaac said. "Including the dead ones."

"Oh, shit," Carl said, his breath quickening. "This is it. This is what we need. We need all of these files."

"But is there anything in there about where they're being kept?" Heather asked.

"I don't know yet," Isaac said. "I'll keep looking."

"Time's up," Carl said. "I've got to call this in. I've got to get this place raided right now."

"Do you need me to punch you or something?" Isaac asked.

Carl stared at Isaac. "Why would you do that?" he asked.

"So you have a story about how we got away?" Isaac said, carefully, as though he didn't understand why Carl was asking.

"No," Carl said. "Don't ever touch me."

Carl took his phone out and started to dial the station, not sure where to begin. With Burgess still in the hospital, he wasn't even sure who to talk to. But, somebody had to have found Banks in holding by now, so there should be plenty of people wanting to talk to him.

"Bad guys are here," Osric said, poking his head casually into the room.

"Fuck," Carl said, and shoved the phone back into his pocket. He followed Osric back out into the foyer and peered through the windows.

Four vans had pulled up the front of the building, completely blocking any view of the door from the street. The doors of the vans opened and a dozen angry-looking skinheads climbed out along with four older men wearing cheap wool suits.

"I don't see any wolves," Carl said, trying to find one good thing about being trapped and outnumbered.

"It's broad daylight," Osric said. "The wolves are probably taking the tunnels."

Carl blinked. "You mean the tunnels that you used to come in?" he asked.

"Yup," Osric said. "Same ones."

"Did you guys lock the door when you came in?" Carl asked.

Osric seemed to think about it for a moment. "I think

so," he said. "Yeah, probably."

"Maybe we should go down there and check," Carl said.

Osric shrugged. "That could get us killed, but okay."

* * *

The door looked every bit as ostentatious as a secret club's secret door into an underground tunnel system would look. Ornate carvings around the frame depicted kneeling knights and bolts of sunlight behind crosses. The door itself displayed a detailed carving of battle between medieval armies under an eclipse. Carl wondered if this was in reference to some little-known bit of Freemason history, or if it was some sort of obscure heraldic code for "don't tell anyone this door is here." Despite conspiracy theorists' claims, The Freemasons had never been involved in domestic terrorism, so Carl knew diddly-squat about them.

Carl and Osric had bounded down two flights of stairs, clearly built several decades apart from each other, to where they abruptly ended at the door. Mercifully, the metal latch was slid down into place, preventing the door from being opened from the other side.

"See?" Osric said. "Nothing to worry--"

A violent thump pushed the door inward and made the metal latch do its work.

"Okay," Carl said, "we both knew that was going to happen. Will this latch hold?"

A second and third thump followed almost immediately. The metal latch strained under the attack, but held.

"I mean," Osric said, "it was built by The Freemasons, but it's also a hundred years old, so…"

Carl nodded. "Let's find something to brace it."

The two of them ran back up the second flight of stairs to the banquet hall. Carl had only glanced at it as they'd gone down, but now that he stood in it, he could see that his first impressions were correct; like the door, it was exactly what one would expect from a secret society's underground banquet hall. To call it cliché would only be ignoring the likelihood that this room was what all the clichés were built on.

A single long, polished wood table stretched down the middle of the room, lined with polished wooden chairs that were somehow even more ornate than the check-out-our-secret-door extravaganza. The walls around them were lined with hanging tapestries, and at the far end of the room, three ceiling-high flagpoles displayed an American flag, a Confederate flag, and a Nazi flag.

"Hey Isaac," Osric yelled up to the ground floor. "There's a couple of Nazi flags down here. You wanna burn 'em?"

"I'm a little busy right now," Isaac's voice called back down. "But, thank you for thinking of me."

"More for us," Osric said, and darted forward towards the flags.

"I'm all for this," Carl said, "but I think we need to stay focused on the invading horde?"

"I can do both," Osric said, grabbing the flagpole that held the Nazi flag.

Ripping the flag off its rings and throwing it towards the table, Osric twisted the flagpole in circles, unscrewing it from its base.

Carl rolled his eyes at himself; of course that was the plan. With the stairs directly in front of the door, they'd be able to brace the flag poles directly between the door and the steps. It would take another hundred years for them to break the door down then.

Carl quickly tore down the Confederate flag and started twisting its pole out of the base. One pole would probably do the trick, but why not make sure.

As they pulled the flag poles from their bases, Carl heard something. It was muffled, so he wasn't sure he'd heard it in the first place. But it was distinctive enough that even moments later, as he and Osric were wedging the flagpoles into place against the rapidly beating door, there was something in the back of his mind that couldn't stop thinking, what was that sound?

"Did you hear that sound earlier?" Carl finally asked Osric after the poles were in place.

There were two more hard slams against the door, and then it went silent. Presumably, the wolves on the other side noticed that the door had been reinforced and were giving up. For now, at least.

"What sound?" Osric asked.

"I don't know," Carl said. "It was something in the banquet room."

"Well," Osric said, "We have to go back in there anyway. Let's go check it out."

"What do we have to go back in there for?" Carl asked.

"Gotta burn the flags, remember?" Osric said, and scampered pack up the stairs.

Carl followed him. "It's not that I don't appreciate the idea," Carl said, "but there are more immediate concerns."

"We might die here, Carl," Osric said. "I'm not leaving this Earth having left a Nazi flag un-burned."

Osric gathered the Nazi and Confederate flags into a pile in the middle of the table, the removed a small plastic bottle with a narrow top from one of his jacket pockets.

"You carry lighter fluid around with you?" Carl asked, as Osric squirted the contents of the bottle over the flags.

"Aren't you glad I do?" Osric said, blankly.

There was the sound again. This time Carl was sure he'd heard it. It was the sound of metal, lightly brushing against itself. It wasn't obvious before, it was coming from behind something, or under something, but now that Carl was listening for it, it was obvious.

It was the sound of chains.

Osric struck a match and set the flags on fire as Carl looked around the room.

"Did you guys look behind the tapestries?" Carl asked.

"We didn't really come in the room," Osric said. "We basically went straight upstairs."

Carl grabbed hold of one of the tapestries and tried to pull it back. It was basically a fifty-pound carpet hung from the ceiling, and wasn't something to just be flourished to one side like silk drapes. Carl ended up having to walk around it to peer at the wall behind it.

Sure enough, it wasn't a wall. There was a door.

Carl pulled his phone out and turned on the flashlight; behind each of the eight tapestries was a padlocked door.

"Can you kick through a padlock?" Carl asked.

"Only one way to find out," Osric said, and with as much direct swiftness as he had upstairs, his foot crashed against the door. The door boomed like it had been hit by a sledgehammer, but did not give way.

"That's a no," Osric said. "Can you shoot the lock off?"

Carl leaned in and listened to the door. He could hear them more clearly now; the tinkling sound of metal chains moving about.

"Is there somebody in there?" Carl called through the

door. "I'm Special Agent Carl Abrams of the FBI."

There was no response from inside. The metal-on-metal sounds of the chains died down. Whoever was in there either didn't know, or wasn't a fan of the FBI.

"I'm not firing my gun at that door," Carl said. "I'm pretty sure there's somebody in there. Look around for a crowbar or something. We need to---Oh shit, the table's on fire!"

"Oh, shit!" Osric exclaimed.

"Quick, pull down the tapestry!" Carl yelled.

The two of them managed to rip the tapestry off of whatever had fastened it to the ceiling's rafters, and they hoisted it over the table to smother the fire.

"Okay, now we find a crowbar," Carl said.

"I think I saw--" Osric began, but was interrupted when the flames burst out from under the tapestry and quickly engulfed it.

"Fuck!" Carl yelled. "What the hell kind of lighter fluid did you use?"

"I don't know!" Osric yelled back. "Tunder made it!"

"Do you see a fire extinguisher anywhere?" Carl yelled, frantically looking around the room.

"It's a secret Nazi clubhouse!" Osric yelled, pulling down another tapestry to throw over the first. "They don't respect the fire codes here! Pull down more tapestries! We have to smother it!"

"We tried that!" Carl yelled back. "That only made it more angry!"

"Just pull down the fucking tapestries!" Osric roared, and Carl complied. Between the two of them, they yanked down the remaining six tapestries and piled them onto the flaming table, leaving all eight padlocked doors around the room newly exposed.

Once the table of flames was completely covered, Carl and Osric stood over it, catching their breath as they waited to see if the fire would break out from under the massive pile of fabric.

"There might be a crowbar upstairs," Osric said, once he was able to. "One of the rooms looked like a workshop or something."

"Cool," Carl said. "Let's go check it out."

"Um," Osric interrupted, before Carl could move. "Please don't tell Heather I yelled at you."

"Seriously?" Carl said.

"There's enough going on," Osric said. "She doesn't need to worry about me losing my temper on top of everything else."

"Is it okay if I tell her you set the table on fire?" Carl asked, smirking. "Or will you get grounded?"

"You can't prove that was my fault," Osric said.

* * *

"What are they doing now?" Carl asked as he topped the stairs to the ground floor with Osric close behind him.

"Notes on a page," Heather said, peering through the windows. "Not a pleasant song."

"We've got civilian traffic now," Isaac said. "I don't think they want to bring attention to themselves, so they're just waiting."

"It's in a minor key," Heather said, "but the meter is all off."

"Is she okay?" Carl asked.

"Yeah, she's fine," Isaac said. "Why?"

Carl stepped up to the front windows to look out. Sure enough, the front of the building was practically walled off by the row of vans parked on the street. Each had their side doors wide open with three or four disgruntled looking men loitering next to them. They were trying to look like every-day citizens just having a chat on the sidewalk, but a trained eye would see they had a full flanking formation, ready to block anyone who tried to make a run from the front doors. In the middle of it all was an especially ghoulish-looking man. He was shorter than most of them, and definitely the oldest among them. He looked like a creepy priest in a horror movie about creepy priests. He stood nearly motionless at the foot of the walkway leading up to the main door, a satisfied look on his face, as though everything was going according to his plan.

Asshole, Carl thought. *Definitely an asshole.*

"They're waiting for the wolves to come in through the tunnels," Osric said. "We sealed the door."

"Nice," Isaac said. "You burn the flags?"

"Yeah," Osric said, "and we need to talk to Tunder about that lighter fluid he gave us."

"He never said it was lighter fluid," Isaac said. "He said it was for starting fires."

"Is our backup coming?" Heather asked.

"Shit," Carl said, digging his phone out of his pocket. "I still haven't called this in."

"Jesus, Carl," Osric mumbled.

"You set the dining hall on fire!" Carl snapped back, pressing the call button on his phone.

"Oh, that reminds me," Osric said, turning to Heather. "We found more doors. They were behind the tapestries. I need a crowbar."

"I think I saw one in here," Heather said, leading Osric off to another room.

"Special Crimes Unit," a voice answered on Carl's phone. "Detective Holcomb speaking."

Carl knew Det. Holcomb. He was one of the detectives in Burgess' unit. Carl wasn't sure what his recent caseload looked like, but he knew it was keeping him busy enough that he hadn't been involved in the case he and Burgess were working on. Carl had only seen him in passing as they both worked in the office, but he seemed like a proper cop for the most part.

"This is Special Agent Carl Abrams," Carl said.

"Abrams," Holcomb said. "Where the fuck are you? People are going nuts here!"

"I know, I know," Carl said. "Burgess is in the hospital, but he should be okay. We were attacked last night."

"You were attacked?" Holcomb said. "Banks says you attacked him."

"Banks is a Neo-Nazi," Carl said. "I caught him trying to clean up the evidence our attackers left behind. Don't let him leave the building."

"Don't let him leave the building?" Holcomb said. "He's on the top floor right now filing a formal complaint. He and the chief are probably on the phone with your office right now."

"Look," Carl said, "I have evidence for all of this, but I need help right now. I have suspects on the kidnapped kids we were tracking, I have evidence of other kidnappings, and even some deaths. But I need a SWAT team to come save my life first, because I'm surrounded by Werewolves!"

"Werewolves?" Holcomb said, skeptically.

"A gang of White Supremacists that call themselves The

Werewolves," Carl said. "There's historical precedence, look it up!"

"I don't command the SWAT," Holcomb said. "I'm going to have to give the chief something other than 'werewolves' to get that authorized. And right now he's on the team that you've gone off the deep end. You locked Banks in a holding cell and disappeared into the night. What did you think was going to happen?"

Carl clenched his jaw. Holcomb was right; this wasn't just against protocol, it was completely insane. Even if he could transmit the files they'd found to them, without context they were worthless; nothing on there saying "Secret Kidnapping Files, Do Not Copy!" Even if Burgess was awake, he probably wouldn't be able to get authorization for this.

"Fine," Carl said. "You all think I've gone nuts, let's go with that. I have a bomb, and I'm about to blow up a building. I'll text you the address."

Carl ended the call and shoved the phone in his pocket as Isaac looked on, astonished.

"Baller move there, G-Man," Isaac said.

"I'm probably already fired," Carl said. "Might as well make a meal out of it."

"Does that mean I can keep the skull now?" Isaac asked.

"Absolutely not," Carl said. "It belongs in a museum."

"Guys," Heather's voice barked behind them.

They turned to see her at the top of the stairs leading down, her face red from racing up the two flights.

"You need to come down here!" She panted. "They're here! We found the kids, they're all here!"

In an instant, all three of them were back down in the dining hall. Osric had crowbarred the locks off all the doors and swung them wide open. Carl skidded to a stop and peered into the first door. Sure enough, there they were. A dozen or so kids, boys and girls, sitting cross-legged on the floor in makeshift nests of dirty blankets and limp pillows, and chained to the wall with padlocked dog collars around their necks. They all looked to be between the ages of seven to ten years old, and were dressed in matching white t-shirts and shorts like the kind you could buy in packs of twenty at an outlet store. None of them looked like they'd been bathed in days, and most of them had some form of bruise or healed-over cut somewhere on them; even at this age they were being sent into the pit to fight each other. All of them peered back at Carl, a mixture of curiosity and suspicion on their faces. None of them made a sound.

Moving to each door, Carl saw the same thing over and over, with only the grouped ages of the children changing, but none of them seemed to have anyone under the age of six.

"This isn't all of them," Carl said. "The infants and toddlers aren't here."

"Maybe they're only brought here when they reach fighting age," Osric said, grimly.

"Look at them," Heather whispered, "they don't even want to leave. They don't even know what's being done to them."

Carl pointed his phone's camera into one of the rooms and snapped a picture.

"If this doesn't get me the SWAT team," Carl said, "I don't know what will."

Carl typed the building address into the phone, attached the photo, and emailed it to the department address that Burgess ran. That would get it to Holcomb, as well as every other member of Burgess' team.

Carl took a deep breath, trying to quiet his mind as he assessed the situation. There were several dozen kidnapped children chained to the walls, stacks of files on all of the kidnapped or killed children, who-knows-how-many toddlers and infants still unaccounted for, a small army of Neo-Nazis camped out at the front door, and an unknown number or sadistic teenagers who think they're werewolves at the back door. On the other side of the board was a psychic girl, her Panzer Tank boyfriend, her comic relief boyfriend, a polymath in a permanent mask named Tunder, and (fingers crossed) the local police.

Carl was miraculously calm. That primal scream had worked wonders for him. Why hadn't he tried that before?

"Now we stall them," Carl said.

"Stall them how?" Isaac asked.

"For how long?" Osric asked.

"Any way we can," Carl said. "For as long as we can."

As though waiting for its cue, an aggressive sound rose up and floated over them from the stairs leading to the tunnel door.

"The music is starting," Heather said, grimly.

"Sounds like a chainsaw," Osric said.

"Right," Isaac said, slumping his shoulders. "Because they're not actual werewolves. They can use tools."

"Did you actually think--?" Carl started to say to Isaac, but thought better of it. "Never mind. No time. Everyone upstairs."

The four of them bounded up to the ground floor, the sound of the chainsaw getting louder behind them as it started to tear into the ancient door.

Not wasting any time, Carl drew his gun as he ran down the hallway and into the library. Not even pausing to second guess himself, he brought the butt of his gun down on the display case as hard as he could, smashing the glass into a shower of jagged edges. As fast he could, not caring if he cut himself as he did, Carl dug the important-looking book from under the threatening maw of the wolf skull and ran back to the front window with it in hand.

The creepy man had not moved from his spot. He still stood at the foot of the path with the frozen look of smug satisfaction. Once Carl was sure the creepy man was watching, he pulled his lighter from his pocket, flicked a flame to life, and held it and the book aloft at the window for the creepy man to see.

The effect was immediate. The creepy man's face went from smug to horrified faster than Carl could blink. He had gotten his attention.

"Call off your dogs!" Carl shouted, hoping that he could be heard even through the muffle of the closed window.

He was. The creepy man turned and shouted something to the men behind him. One of them immediately began shouting orders into a cell phone, and seconds later the sound of the chainsaw went quiet.

"Okay, how come *you* get to take things?" Isaac said.

CHAPTER ELEVEN
A MORAL BANKRUPTCY

The creepy guy glared at Carl as he approached the window, like a cartoon villain getting ready to really lay into one of his henchmen. Carl held steady, keeping the book just above the flame of his lighter.

The man stopped just short of the window and spoke. His voice was muffled by the thick glass in the well-sealed window frame. Carl thought he could barely make out the words "do you even know what you have there?" with all manner of sinister obstinance dripping from it.

"What?" Carl shouted at the window. "I can't hear you!"

"Do you even know what you're holding?" the man said, louder this time. Carl could hear him this time, but it was clear that the man was trying not to yell at full volume. He was still concerned about unwanted attention from the public in the streets. That was good.

"Nope, sorry!" Carl shouted, waving one had at his ears like he still couldn't hear anything. "You need to project! From the diaphragm!"

The creepy man twitched, but he didn't break. Whatever

it was that Carl was threatening to burn, it was important enough to keep a Nazi polite.

The man turned over his shoulder and said something to one of his men. One of them brought him a cell phone.

"Christ," Carl said to Heather, watching the man place his call. "He even dials a phone like an asshole."

A phone rang somewhere in the building. Carl was pretty sure it was coming from the office, but he didn't move to investigate. He stood in place at the window, keeping the book and lighter in full view of the men outside.

"I'll get it," Isaac said. "It might be for me." It took a lot out of Carl to keep from chuckling. He couldn't break in front of the Nazi any more than the Nazi could break in front of him.

"Thank you for calling Werewolf Headquarters," Carl could hear Isaac say from the office, in exactly the tone one would expect from a Hotel Desk Clerk. "How may I direct your call?"

"Put the Jew on the phone," the creepy guy said. Carl had no problem making that one out through the glass, but he still managed to keep his cool.

"I'm sorry, I don't have anyone here by that name," Isaac replied, with almost sing-song professionalism. "Perhaps you should check who's holding your precious book and try again."

Carl waved the lighter lightly under the book to emphasize Isaac's point. The Creepy Nazi's face twitched again, but still held firm.

"Agent Abrams, please," he finally said. Even through the muffle of the window, Carl could hear the growl in his voice.

"And may I tell him who's calling?" Issac asked.

"My name is Arthur Remus," the creepy old nazi said.

"That's my school you're occupying."

"Carl!" Isaac shouted from the office. "It's for you. I think it's that asshole you were talking about."

"I'm a little preoccupied at the moment," Carl called back, not breaking eye contact with Remus. "Can you bring the phone over here?"

"Nah," Isaac replied. "It's one of those shitty old ones that's plugged into the wall. You'd think The Master Race could've gone cordless by now."

"Tell 'em to call back, then." Carl said.

Remus obviously could hear their exchange though the phone; his face was turning beet red even before Isaac replied to him.

"I'm sorry, Agent Abrams can't come to the phone right now," Isaac said. "If you have a message, I can deliver it to him in The 21st Century."

"There's a cordless phone in the workshop," Remus said through gritted teeth.

"Where in the workshop?" Isaac asked.

"It's mounted on the wall by the door," Remus said. "You can't miss it."

"Please hold," Isaac said. Carl's staring contest with the Nazi continued as he could hear Isaac strolling from one room to another behind him. A moment later, he strode back and picked the receiver back up off the desk.

"It's not in there," Isaac said. "It wasn't on its cradle."

"Did you look around for it?" Remus spat into the phone. Carl thought he would faint from the effort of holding back his laughter.

"Don't take that tone with me, Mr. Nazi," Isaac said. "I'm not the one who can't put his things away."

Remus dropped the phone from his ear and covered the

mouthpiece, looking for a moment like he wanted to scream before taking a breath and lifting the phone back up.

"Check the library," he said. "It ends up in there sometimes."

"We were just in the library," Isaac said. "I didn't see it there."

"Check again," Remus growled. "It might be in one of the drawers."

"Alright," Isaac said, sounding bored. Carl appreciated the effort Isaac was making to antagonize the racist fascists, but his arms were getting tired. He was rooting for things to hurry along now, but he couldn't show it as long as the racist fascist was watching.

"Oh, here it is," Isaac said, followed by a short beep as he activated the handset. "Are you there?"

"Yes, I'm here," Remus said.

"Okay, I'm going to put you on speaker," Isaac said, strolling into the foyer with the phone. There was another beep as Isaac stepped up to Carl's side and held the phone up to him.

"Jew speaking," Carl said.

"Do you even know what you're holding?" Remus asked.

"No idea," Carl said. "But I don't need to know what it is to know it's important to you."

"If anything happens to that book," the creepy nazi growled, "there will be no place on this earth you can hide."

"Oh whatever, Chucklehead," Carl said. "I've put a hundred guys like you away already, and it's starting to bore me. Why don't we just skip to the part where you surrender?"

"Surrender?" Remus spat. "To you?"

"If you want to avoid the Death Penalty, yeah," Carl said.

"I've got your book, your records, and most of your kids. All you've got is the location of the babies. If you give that up, you *might* be allowed to live out the rest of your natural days. But only if one of your thugs back there doesn't beat you to it."

"What makes you think any of that is ever getting out of this building?" Remus asked.

"What makes you think it hasn't already?" Carl asked.

"Because none of your Deep State friends have come to save you," Remus smirked.

"Oh," Carl said, shaking his head. "Nobody was ever coming to save me. I'm not the one you have to worry about."

"What do you mean?" Remus furrowed his brow.

Right on cue, Heather stepped up to the window so she could be seen by Remus and his friends for the first time. She held Carl's phone up to show the photo of the chained-up kids that Carl had snapped earlier.

"I just posted this photo to every Internet Mom Group I could find," she said, smiling broadly. "As we speak, every phone at every law enforcement agency for fifty miles is blowing up with demands for an armed incursion."

The creepy nazi didn't react much, but considering how stoic he'd been up to that point, any reaction at all meant he was going out of his mind.

"Oh, I guess while we're talking," Isaac said, "I should probably point out that while my brother was setting fire to your flags downstairs, I was sending images of your files to a freelance reporter we know. He'll make sure you get headlines within an hour."

Now Remus was visibly shaking, but still not making a move.

Just then, Carl's phone buzzed, making Heather jump.

"Oh," she said. "It's a message from Tunder."

"About time," Carl said. "What's it say?"

"The DNA matched four open murder cases from the last two years," Heather said, paraphrasing the message. "And he found an uncle, so we'll know her real name in a couple of hours."

"Did he do Phase Two?" Carl asked.

Heather scanned through the message again. "Oh, you mean the part where he traced back the accounts that were paying the utility bills for this building and got them frozen? Yeah, he says he did that."

"Cool," Carl said, "tell him I said thanks."

"You're dead," Remus hissed through the phone. "You're all dead."

"No, I think you're dead," Carl said. "This isn't your book, is it?"

The worn-out skinhead went from red to white in record time. In the whole spectrum of emotions Carl had seen this guy go through in the last five minutes, this was the most purely terrified he'd seen.

"We've been sitting here telling you how fucked you are. There is no escape for you anymore, and you haven't budged. Not to come at us, and not to run." Carl said. "It's because I've still got the book, isn't it? You said there'd be no place on Earth I could hide, but that's actually you, isn't it? If something happens to this book, someone you're scared of more than anything is going to make you pay for it, aren't they?"

Remus didn't say anything. He just stood frozen in place, seeming to get even whiter by the second.

"That's a really good point," Isaac said. "Can I see that

book?"

"Not now," Carl hissed at Isaac, still not breaking eye-contact with Remus. "Turn yourself in, tell us where the rest of the kids are, and we can protect you."

"You really have no idea," the creepy nazi said, "the hornets nest you're kicking right now."

"I've kicked hornets nests before," Carl said, calmly. "I've poked bears. I've woken dragons. Even dated a Scorpio once. You don't scare me."

"Not me," Remus snarled. "You pathetic globalist whore. The sheer number of terrors that are about to reign down on you and your--"

"Boring!" Carl shouted. "Do all you assholes shop at the same Vague Threat Store? Is that why this book is so important? Is this the original 'Your Worst Nightmare' speech book?"

Remus fell silent, closing his eyes and taking a breath.

"Do you even care," he asked, "that you're robbing these children of their destiny?"

"Their destiny?" Carl asked. "To be stolen from their families and made to fight each other to the death? That's a pretty sick destiny, if you ask me?

"The world as you know it is on the cusp of a rebirth," Remus said. "When that day comes, they will be the harbingers of the New Order."

"Right," Carl said. "That Race War you people have been itching over for decades. They're supposed to be your new Storm Troopers, I take it?"

"Not a Race War," Remus said. "Something much more. A paradigm shift that you or I can't even grasp yet. But yes, they will be the front lines, and they will be heralded as heroes in the next life. Taking them from this place means dooming them to the same oblivion as you."

"What about the ones who failed?" Isaac asked. It was the first time Carl had heard him speak with any true seriousness. It took him aback for a moment.

"What about them?" Remus asked.

"I counted over two-hundred files in your office," Isaac said. "But there's only about thirty kids downstairs. What happened to the rest of them? Was it their destiny to be your fodder?"

"Only the strongest are allowed to ascend," Remus said.

"You mean the most cruel," Carl said. "Because that's really the point to all of this. You're making those children into monsters."

"If you knew what was coming," Remus said, "you know that it was necessary."

It was faint at first, but it only took a second for Carl's brain to identify the sound. The beautiful, glorious sound of police sirens, lots of them, heading their way. Remus heard them too, suddenly looking away from Carl and towards the street. The view was still blocked by the row of vans, but one-by-one you could see it on the faces of all the Nazi Thugs standing there; The Fuzz was closing in.

"Speaking of what's coming" Carl said, grinning.

Remus turned his attention back to the window just in time to see Carl touch the flame of his lighter to the book, lighting it up.

"No!" Remus screamed, dropping his phone to the ground and slamming his palms against the window in fury. "What have you done? Have you lost your mind?"

"Honestly," Carl said, dropping the flaming book to the floor, "I just wanted to see the look on your face."

With that, Remus spun around and said something they

couldn't hear to the men gathered behind him. It was rather obvious what he said, though. They all immediately produced handguns from concealed holsters and aimed to open fire on the front of the building.

"Down!" Carl shouted, dropping to the floor as gunfire went off and glass shattered above him. As he ducked down, the flames from the still-burning book licked up against him, burning his arm. In a panicked reflex, Carl tried slapping the flames out while gunfire continued to explode around him.

"Osric!" Heather yelled, pressed against the floor just inside the doorway to the library. "Where's Osric?!"

"I don't know!" Isaac replied, yelling over the gunfire.

"Stay down!" Carl yelled. "Don't try to move!"

The gunfire stopped as abruptly as it started. In the sudden quiet, Carl could hear the sirens much closer now. Police cruisers were on the street and filling up the block around the building. A new round of gunfire started going off, this time not at them. The pop-pop noise wasn't followed by exploding glass or wood around them; the Nazis had turned their fire towards the cops.

That was when Carl heard another sound; the sound of the chainsaw down below. The wolves were on their way in again, and with the police force being held at bay outside, Carl had no defense against them.

"Stay here!" Carl yelled at Isaac and Heather as he bolted for the stairs. He may not be able to stop them, but if he could slow them down long enough for the SWAT to break through, then the others would be okay.

He bounded down the stairs as fast as he could, jumping down as many steps at a time as he could. He cleared the first flight to the dining hall in only six steps, and stopped there to draw his gun and chance a glance towards the doors that lead to the scores of chained-up kids. As cruel as it had been to keep them chained this whole time, it was at least keeping them out of danger for the moment.

The chainsaw sound abruptly ended, followed by a crashing noise as the last bits of door were kicked in and the flag-pole braces clattered to the ground.

With a deep breath and an acceptance that this may be his last act on Earth, Carl marched down the steps to the door, his gun leveled in front of him.

As he tuned the landing to the last flight, there was Osric, crowbar in hand, standing at the ready only a foot from the door. In the doorway, a wolf that was already tall even before the stilted leg braces were put on him towered over Osric. Even from behind the mask, Carl could see the fury in his eyes as he drew back his metal-clawed hand.

"Get down!" Carl yelled, leveling his weapon on the wolf.

Osric didn't listen. Instead, he swung the crowbar in a low arc and struck the inside of the wolf's groin. The wolf's leg and crotch were covered in strips of armor, but that wasn't where Osric was aiming. The crowbar struck squarely in the crook between the crotch and the leg, where there was no armor. There was an audible crunch as the wolf's hip was shattered.

The wolf's strike went wild and missed Osric completely as it fell to the ground, screaming in pain. Not howling. Not roaring. Screaming.

As that wolf fell to the ground, another was instantly in view in the doorway. This one seemed stunned that its comrade had fallen so succinctly. It took less than a second for it to recover, and it bolted through the door, stepping over its fallen packmate as it did.

As soon as the second wolf stepped through the door,

Osric brought the crowbar down on its knee, and it fell in place as well, also screaming.

Carl realized now what Osric was doing. The door was a bottleneck. It didn't matter how many of them there were, they could only come through the door one at a time, and they barely fit as they did. As long as he didn't move from that spot, he could pile a blockade of broken wolves at the entrance. With each one that fell, the next would be that much more vulnerable as it came in.

Carl lowered his weapon, waiting for a moment when Osric might lose control of the situation and need some gunfire. Carl might actually be able to hit them this time if their attention was focused on Osric.

It was a sight to behold. Osric had clearly taken some sort of fight training at some point in his life. To say he was an expert would be an exaggeration, but Carl knew real skill when he saw it. As a third and fourth wolf stepped through the door, Osric broke their shoulder and ankle, respectively. His movements were tight and controlled, arms kept close to his body, as he spun the crowbar this way and that like a baton twirler in a marching band.

It was the fifth wolf that got wise to what Osric was doing, and instead of stepping over the bodies of its packmates, it took a running leap into the room and landed inches in front of Osric. He was too close for Osric to strike at him without swinging wide first, which would leave him open for a direct attack.

Osric didn't fall for the bait. Instead he took a step back onto the stairs, putting a hand behind him to catch himself from falling. As the wolf swung his clawed hands, Osric swatted the first strike away with the crowbar. But that gave the wolf the opening he was hoping for, and a second swipe with his other hand made contact, leaving four bloody claw marks across Osric's back.

Carl leveled his gun and fired. He was right; the wolf was too focused on Osric to see it coming, and the shot hit him in the chest, just below his shoulder. The wolf reeled backwards and fell over the bodies of the other fallen wolves, joining them in their agonizing wails of pain.

Carl pointed his gun at the darkness past the open door, waiting for another wolf to show themselves, but none did. Either that was the last one, or the rest had realized they were outmatched by a narrow door.

"Everybody shut up!" Carl yelled at the wolves, writhing and crying on the floor. "There will be ambulances on the way. None of you are dying."

"I will bathe in your entrails," a voice groaned from the pile of wolves.

"I have a gun," Carl said. "Stop talking."

"Can I get an ambulance too," Osric said, sitting himself upright. "I can't remember if my Tetanus is up-to-date."

"At least now I know you're not indestructible," Carl said, kneeling down to Osric.

"I never claimed to be," Osric said, resting against the stairway wall, careful not to lean on the wound.

"Whatever happened to rolling with it?" Carl asked, smirking.

"You can't roll with claws, dummy," Osric smirked back.

"Not if you don't practice," Carl said.

"Hands in the air! Nobody move!" a voice boomed at them from above.

Carl turned to see three SWAT team members, guns at the ready, facing down at them from the stairs above.

"FBI!" Carl shouted, raising his hands up, letting his gun

fall loose to one finger so they could see he wasn't going to fire. "I'm FBI! Special Agent Carl Abrams!"

With a tense presentation of identification, the SWAT team finally stood down and let Carl point out to them who the good guys were. As the SWAT team dealt with the injured wolves, Carl led Osric up the stairs. There were SWAT officers and uniformed cops heading into the rooms with the chained up kids, presumably to try and collect them for Child Services, but it seemed to be going about as well as the rest of the raid.

"The little fucker bit me!" Carl heard someone call out as he and Osric continued up to the ground floor.

The streets outside were positively choked with flashing lights. Police cruisers, unmarked official vehicles, SWAT vans, and ambulances filled both lanes for three blocks in both directions, and probably wrapped around the block as well. Carl could barely get his bearings before Heather appeared out of nowhere, wrapping her arms around Osric and wailing.

"I was so worried about you!" she cried, burying her face in his chest.

"I know," he said, trying not to sound like she was causing him as much pain as she was. "I'm sorry. I had to go hit Nazis with a crowbar."

"You didn't think to invite me?" Isaac said, stepping up to them and putting a hand on Osric's shoulder, aware of his injuries.

"What would you have done?" Osric asked.

"Nothing," Isaac said, "but I would've liked to see it."

"What is that, Isaac?" Carl asked, pointing to a large duffel bag that Isaac was holding.

"It's a bag I found in the workshop," Isaac said, flatly. He was clearly hoping that Carl wouldn't ask any follow-up questions.

"Is the wolf skull in there?" Carl asked.

"His name is Madmardigan," Isaac said. "And he doesn't want to be a Nazi anymore."

"Jesus," Carl said, rolling his eyes.

"We need to get you to the hospital," Heather sniffed, finally letting go of him.

"There's ambulances all around," Carl said. "Just pick one."

"We need to take him to *our* hospital," Isaac said. "The one that won't put us in a police report."

"Don't you guys want to be heroes?" Carl asked.

"Unfortunately," Isaac said, "being known as a hero actually makes it hard to keep being one."

"Well, it's not going to be easy," Carl said, looking around at the pandemonium. There were suspects and perps being restrained and carted off, others being loaded into ambulances, others still being zipped up into body bags. "There's a perimeter set up, and you're not going to be able to get to the tunnels anymore."

"Can't you walk us out?" Heather asked.

"Maybe," Carl said. "But I did kind of call in a bomb threat, so I might end up in handcuffs myself any minute now."

"That's an understatement," a voice said behind them.

Carl turned to see a plainclothes cop approaching them. It took Carl a second to recognize him.

"Detective Holcomb," Carl said. "What took you so long?"

"What took us?" Holcomb said, exasperated. "A fucking shootout broke out at the station, you dick!"

"The hell?" Carl said.

"When I went to the chief with the address you sent me, Banks was still with him," Holcomb said. "The guy lost his shit right away. Pulled his piece and tried to shoot his way out. Turns out he had about a half-dozen buddies on the floor with him. The place is a mess now. And even after that went down, a fucking whole new can of worms opened up when news about this place went wide all over the internet. The fucking mayor has been screaming at everybody for an hour straight."

"Is Burgess awake yet?" Carl asked.

"Is Burgess--?" Holcomb sputtered. "Fuck you, man! It's fucking Fallujah out here, and you want---"

Holcomb stopped himself and took a breath.

"Yeah, the lieutenant is awake," he said. "He and his wife are running the Child Services side of things from his hospital room. The only reason I didn't shoot you on sight is because he backed you up."

"I was hoping as much," Carl said, nodding.

"Who the fuck are these guys?" Holcomb asked, waving a finger at Heather and her boys.

"Innocent bystanders," Carl said. "Can you walk them to their car?"

"Are you fucking kidding me?" Holcomb said. "They need to make statements. And that guy needs an ambulance."

"Your mom needs an ambulance," Osric snorted.

"Osric," Carl shushed, then turned back to Holcomb. "I've got these guys. They just need to get out of here. Burgess is already in the loop about them."

Holcomb eyed them suspiciously.

"What's in the bag?" he asked.

"Preserved timber wolf skull," Isaac said. "It's so cool.

177

Do you want to see it?"

"Fuck," Holcomb said. "Follow me, assholes."

Holcomb headed off towards the street. Osric put an arm around Isaac and the two of them hobbled along behind.

"Carl," Heather said, before following them, "we still don't know--"

"I know," Carl said. "Go take care of Osric and get some sleep. I've got it from here."

She nodded. "I believe you this time," she said, and ran off to catch up with her boys.

Carl wanted to collapse onto the ground and sleep for a week where he fell. He had been awake for twenty-six hours, the coffee that Shannon had given him had long since worn off, and the adrenaline was starting to subside. In all honesty, he was starting to feel short on reasons to stay upright.

But there was one good reason. Carl went back into the building and looked around the floor. He found the burnt-up book right where he left it, in even worse shape after being stomped on by who-knows-how-many stampeding officers.

Carl picked it up, brushed it off, and examined it. The cover was burned too badly to read the title anymore, but most of the inside of the book survived. Now that Carl was feeling less frantic, the words almost looked familiar to him. The book was written in English, but an especially old style of English that he hadn't recognized without taking the time to really examine it. That would make this book more than six-hundred years old. Regardless of its contents, it was an archaeological artifact. Carl suddenly felt very guilty about burning it.

It took some wandering around, but Carl finally found Arthur Remus handcuffed to a gurney, an oxygen mask over his face and a uniformed officer recited the Miranda Rights to him.

"I'd like a word," Carl said to the officer.

"He hasn't lawyered up yet," the officer said. "Knock yourself out."

Carl took a seat inside the ambulance, looking down on Remus' scowling face.

"What's his name?" Carl asked.

Remus didn't speak. He stared coldly back up at Carl.

"It's the kid, right?" Carl said. "The one in the photo in your office. He's all grown up now and makes you shit your pants, is that right? Tell me his name."

Remus still didn't talk. He rolled his eyes at Carl and turned away from him.

"You're already fucked," Carl said. "What have you got to lose?"

"Which name do you want?" Remus said, his voice muffled by the oxygen mask. "The one he's using today, or the one he'll use when he comes for you?"

"Why not both," Carl said. "I'm feeling feisty."

"He is the Favored Son of The Seven Fathers," Remus said. "They each gave him a name."

"So, he has seven identities," Carl said. "That's handy. What are they?"

"I don't know," Remus said. "He doesn't like it when anyone but his fathers speak the names they gave him."

"Sounds like a real prince," Carl said. "But I guess it's neither here nor there. I'll have plenty of time in an interrogation room with you soon enough. I was just curious."

Carl pulled the burnt book from his pocket and held it up for Remus to see. He got the reaction he wanted; Remus' eyes widening at the sight of the book still in one piece.

"My next question is time sensitive, however," Carl said. "Where are the rest of the fucking kids?"

CHAPTER TWELVE
CLOSING THE BOOK

The hospital was refusing to discharge Burgess until he'd been under observation for 24-hours. When Carl arrived that evening, Burgess looked absolutely miserable to be stuck in bed while all the excitement was still buzzing around the city.

"I can't believe you let him keep the skull," Burgess said, after Carl spun the whole tale.

"I know," Carl breathed, exasperated with himself. "I shouldn't have done that. I'm going to blame it on sleep deprivation."

"You heard from them since?" Burgess asked.

"No," Carl said. "They're probably all still asleep in their little mud thatch, or hobbit hole, or whatever weirdos live in. I'm surprised I haven't passed out yet."

"You get any sleep at all?" Burgess asked.

"I've caught a power nap here and there," Carl said, "between interrogations. I'm kind of afraid that once I do let myself really sleep it may be days before I wake up."

"I know that feeling," Burgess nodded. "No reason to put

it off, though. Still a long road ahead sorting all of this mess out."

"Yeah," Carl said. "Not for me, though."

"What?" Burgess said, quizzically.

"I fly back to D.C. in the morning," Carl said. "I'm being pulled off the case."

"The hell you say," Burgess said. "Why?"

"Just like they said they would," Carl said. "This is a White Power operation, so I'm being replaced with someone still on the Task Force. They're probably just going to say it was a hundred lone cases of mental illness and leave. Meanwhile, I've got about a hundred years of disciplinary hearings to get started on."

"Jesus christ," Burgess said. "Don't worry, I'll make sure it all gets straightened out."

"I appreciate it," Carl nodded. "But honestly, I don't think I care about any of that anymore. I'm just glad we got all the kids back."

"Yeah, those kids," Burgess said, not sounding reassured. "That's a whole 'nother mess of its own."

"I don't envy you there," Carl said. "Has there been any luck in locating the parents of the replacement kids?"

"Nothing but dead ends," Burgess said. "These poor kids came out of the ether. Most of them are ending up staying with the families they were in. Probably going to end up getting adopted. So, that's a mercy."

"How about the kids we rescued?" Carl asked. "Have they been reunited with their families yet?"

"Some," Burgess said. "We're having a heck of a time identifying them. None of them have been very cooperative. They were all raised to think that being treated like a dog by a bunch of Skinheads is perfectly normal. Some of them are refusing to eat because they don't trust the food we're giving them. It's fuckin' heartbreaking. And that's just the younger ones. The older kids...Jesus I can't even think about it."

"Fully programmed and uncooperative?" Carl asked.

"That's putting it mildly," Burgess said. "They're not just programmed, they've been looking forward to joining the fight along with the costumed freaks that attacked us last night. They're prisoners of war as far as they're concerned."

"You think they can be helped?" Carl asked. "Not just them, but the ones who attacked us. They were just kids, after all. Maybe they can be reformed."

"I'd like to think so," Burgess said, "but between you, me, and the wall, I don't have high hopes for them."

"Why do you say that?" Carl asked.

"Because they're the survivors," Burgess said. "These kids were made to fight and kill each other while they were growing up. If you're not totally on board with the Master Plan, excited by it even, you wouldn't live very long in that place. Those kids in the masks, and the older ones in the chains, they got as old as they did by being the most vicious of their peers. They weren't just surviving in that place, they were thriving in it, and they murdered the ones who didn't. My wife would chew me out for saying this, but I think they might be lost causes."

"Fuck, that's depressing," Carl said, thinking back to Heather's half-conscious recollection of Tyler Sykes living the last months of his life in fear, knowing he was about to die. Carl didn't want to let it on to Burgess, but that was the real reason he was afraid to go to sleep. Now that he'd seen with his own eyes what had happened to the children, he was pretty sure he was going to have nightmares for the rest of his life.

"But I guess we're going to try anyway," Burgess said. "If we didn't at least try, then we'd be just as bad as the Nazis."

"No, the Nazis are definitely worse," Carl said. "But I get your point."

"You think you'll ever want to set foot in Landfall again?" Burgess asked, masterfully changing the subject to something measurably less uncomfortable.

"If the job brings me here again, sure," Carl said.

"No interest in sticking around longer than you have to, huh?" Burgess said.

"I don't know," Carl said. "There's something about this place. I think you might be wrong about it."

"Wrong how?" Burgess asked.

"The other night," Carl said, "when you said the city isn't as weird as it seems. I don't think that's correct. I think it might be a little weirder than it seems."

"What do you mean?" Burgess pressed.

"Did you know that locals can use the tunnels?" Carl said.

"What?" Burgess furrowed his brow.

"That's how our friends broke into the building," Carl said. "They went through the tunnels. And that's how those kids got around the town in those wolf getups without anyone ever seeing them. According to those three weirdos, the trick is to be born here."

"You're fucking with me," Burgess said.

"Saw it with my own eyes," Carl said. "From Point A to Point B, no trouble."

"I'm going to have to talk to some people about this," Burgess said.

"But you see what I'm getting at, right?" Carl said. "As weird as this place already seems on the surface, I think it gets a lot weirder if you start to really look at it. And, honestly, I can't tell if I find that intriguing or terrifying."

"Your new friends didn't explain it to you or anything?" Burgess asked.

"Didn't really have time to get into it," Carl said.

"Yeah, well," Burgess grumbled, "I'll definitely be getting to the bottom of that."

Carl was quiet for a moment. He had been debating with himself for the whole day whether it should be said out loud. Maybe it was just exhaustion, or maybe the total wackiness of the situation was starting to mess with his head, but there was one thing that was really screwing up his head.

"That's not even the weirdest thing," Carl finally said.

"No?" Burgess asked.

"You know how I said the frat building was unguarded?" Carl asked.

"Yeah," Burgess said.

"It wasn't supposed to be," Carl said. "Found out through interrogations, that there were supposed to be two guys there babysitting the kids."

"Where the hell were they?" Burgess asked.

"On their way to the Emergency Room," Carl said. "One of them got food poisoning and was puking his guts out. They figured the kids would be fine alone for an hour or so, so the other guy drove them to the E.R. They left so quickly, they didn't even bother to make sure the door to the tunnels was locked."

"So, what?" Burgess asked. "Somebody poisoned their food to get them out of the way?"

"Nope," Carl said, "I checked. It was an honest-to-goodness bad turkey sandwich."

"Wow," Burgess said, "that's lucky."

"Yeah, lucky," Carl said. "If it weren't for that, this whole thing would've fallen apart. The only reason I got into that building was because the three wackadoodles let me in. If not for them, Banks would've gotten the place cleared out before I could get a warrant. We would've lost all the kids and had nothing to go on, and I probably would've had my badge pulled right then and there."

"Yeah," Burgess said. "Like I said; lucky."

"Is it though?" Carl said. "I mean, I don't believe any of this 'psychic' shit, but…"

"Look," Burgess said, "this thing is all tangled up right now. By the time we're done working it out, I'm sure it'll be pretty obvious where she got her info."

"Yeah maybe," Carl said, "but I can't help but wonder. Why now? Twenty years these people have been at this, so why did we get the heads up about it when we did? We didn't just get a tip-off, we got a tip-off at the exact moment when we could do the most good with it, right down to the hour. We saved all the kids, and rounded up all the Nazis, because we found out about them just in time for one guy to get food poisoning."

Burgess was quiet, either deep in thought or deeply worried about Carl's state of mind.

"That," Carl said, jamming his finger against the railing of the hospital bed for emphasis, "is fucking *weird*."

Burgess took a contemplative breath, before speaking. "You should probably get some sleep," he said.

* * *

The next morning, as Carl was checking out of the hotel, he was surprised to see Isaac at the Front Desk as though it were a normal day.

186

"What are you doing here?" Carl said, once he was sure there were no other guests to overhear them. "After everything that went down yesterday, I'd think you'd want a day off."

"Gotta keep up my secret identity," Isaac said with a proud grin.

"How are, uh, you know," Carl asked, not sure how to phrase it.

"My half-brother and our girlfriend?" Isaac said it for him. "You can say it. I say it all the time."

"Yeah, them," Carl said, still not sure what to make of that situation. "How are they?"

"Heather's doing better," Isaac said. "Having this whole thing wrapped up really helped. She got a full night's sleep. Osric got a couple hundred stitches in his back and has done nothing but complain since. After my shift is done today, I'm going to spend the weekend playing video games. We are about as close to normal as our kind can get."

"Just like that," Carl said, "once his stitches are out it'll be like it never happened for any of you?"

"Well," Isaac said, "probably not so simple as that. But, mostly, yeah. We wanted to help, and we helped. All things considered, it was a good day for us. We're probably not even going to wait for Osric to fully heal before we're on to the next one."

"Is that healthy?" Carl asked. "You may think you signed up for it, but you can't deny that what you went through was traumatic."

Isaac cocked his head to one side, a curiously look in his eye.

"Are we still talking about me, G-Man?" he asked.

"What?" Carl said, taken aback.

"You've been at this job a lot longer than we have," Isaac said. "Just because you've got a badge and a gun doesn't mean you're any less human than we are. How many days are you going to take off before your next case?"

"It's my job," Carl said. "I was trained for this."

"You weren't trained for *this*, Carl," Isaac said. "This was fucking weird."

"Yeah," Carl said, suddenly feeling uncomfortably vulnerable. "Yeah, it was fucking weird."

"You still got the phone we gave you?" Isaac asked.

"Yeah," Carl said. He knew he should have thrown it in the river as soon as they were out of his sight, but he kept telling himself that he should hold on to it, just in case. It was a convenient, comforting excuse; Just in case.

"Why don't you hold on to it," Isaac said. "We'll keep the number active for now. Stay in touch. Call anytime."

"Really?" Carl said. "You want me to call you to talk about my feelings?"

"Remember the presentation I gave you the other night?" Isaac said. "You're a Normal World Person who's just been kicked in the face by the Outside World. As an Oddball, it's my duty to help you adapt to it."

Carl shook his head. "Oddity," he said. "It's a way better word than Oddball."

Isaac thought about it for a second. "Nah," he said, "I like Oddball better."

"Well, you're just plain wrong there," Carl said.

Isaac smiled. "Have a safe trip, G-Man," he said.

Carl nodded silently, and strode out of the hotel.

EPILOGUE

The night before his arraignment, Arthur Remus couldn't sleep. They'd kept him in the hospital for a week before finally releasing him to police custody, and he hadn't known a moment's peace since. Hounded by reporters, questioned by authorities, throngs of protesters screaming for his head. Every few hours he'd be visited by news of yet another of his cohorts turning on him and volunteering testimony.

Remus was sure it was some kind of conspiracy. Surely, once the authorities got involved, he didn't expect things to go well for him from there, but with his advancing age and the injuries he sustained, the hospital was giving him a sense of security. If need be, he could always feign a fainting spell or a weak heart. If he played it right, he could stay in the hospital indefinitely and never see the inside of a courtroom.

Instead, things seemed to work in his favor as the days went by. The media seemed to be unable to get a straight story about what had gone on at his school, and the public was more dumbfounded than anything else. His people were following protocol and keeping their mouths shut. The children, bless them, were making more trouble for the Big Government Bastards than he could have hoped for. It was looking like he'd be able to salvage something from the operation, all he had to do was post bail and resume his leadership. He might still be able to fulfill his duties to The Seven Fathers and reap his rewards.

But then, as he was being escorted from the hospital, practically at the very moment he signed his discharge papers, the dominos began falling. Confessions, bank records, political actions; one by one, everything and everyone he was counting on betrayed him.

And then, there was the book. The book was damaged, and he knew he would face punishment for that, but it was still intact and that was the only thing keeping The Seven Fathers from bringing their full wrath down upon him. If he could get it released from evidence, he might still be able to plead for their help in the coming days. But, bit by bit, it was becoming increasingly clear that it would be kept out of his reach. Someone, possibly that Jew Fed, was keeping the book from him.

And now he sat alone. For fear that there would be an attempt on his life, they hadn't put him in general holding. He instead sat in a holding cell on the fifth floor of Police Headquarters; a bare room with a steel door. In the morning, he would be walked across the street to the courthouse to have the very long list of charges read to him, as though he had any care as to what this false court of godless men thought. He couldn't sleep because all he could think about was the indignity of it all.

The door opened unceremoniously. If there had been any indication that it was about to open, Remus was too lost in thought to notice it, and nearly jumped out of his skin when it did. He had already been given his dinner for the night, and wasn't expecting to see another soul until they came to collect him in the morning. He would occasionally hear an officer wander by the cell and look in to make sure he was still there, but he didn't expect to be disturbed for the rest of the night.

But it wasn't an officer who had opened the door. Remus felt the blood drain from his face as the stone-chiseled eyes of The Favored Son peered down at him.

"I…" Remus stammered. "I can still fix this. I can still recover the book."

"You mean this book?" The Son said, pulling an evidence bag from his pocket with the book still in it. "I came to tell you that I've concluded the audit of your operation."

Remus gulped and looked at the floor.

"Have Your Fathers made their decision?" he asked.

"They have," The Son said. "It's worth saying that they've never been displeased with you. Your dedication is admirable and they appreciate your loyalty. However, your school has ultimately been a failure."

"Failure?" Remus said. "But you've seen them for yourself. My children are the strongest, most--"

"There are eight of them," The Favored Son interrupted. "Out of two-hundred and thirty-five candidates, you've produced only eight successes. You're not just a failure, Mr. Remus. You're an embarrassment."

Remus could feel the breath leaving his body. He knew what all of this meant. In the thirty years he'd been working in service of The Seven Fathers, he'd rendered these punishments himself. As a failure and a disappointment, this was where his story would end.

"I understand," Remus wheezed. "All I ask is that you

make it quick. And when you find that Jew fed, make it slow."

The Son sighed at that, rolling his eyes in the first display of any feelings that Remus had seen from him in almost a decade.

"That's the problem with people like you," The Son said. "You're all so 'Final Solution' about everything. Just because you and Agent Abrams have inconvenienced us, doesn't mean we're going to kill either of you."

"Wh-what?" Remus stammered.

"Killing someone over every little mistake or perceived slight," The Son said. "It's so...*sophomoric*. It's why none of you have ever been able to hold on to power for very long. Real power comes from being able to ignore people like Agent Abrams, and to simply forget about people like you. Agent Abrams could hunt us for the rest of his life. You could tell everyone all about us. None of it will matter. Our plans will continue, The Seal will be broken, and My Fathers and I will rule over the new world. There is nothing anyone can do to change that. *That* is real power."

"You're not here to punish me?" Remus asked, the blood now rushing to his head in relief.

"No, of course not," The Son said. "I told you I was here to tell you that I had concluded your audit."

"Thank you," Remus breathed, at last something was going his way. "Thank you. Thank you."

"Of course," The Son continued, "I don't envy your situation."

"My situation?" Remus asked.

"Prison is not pleasant as it is," The Son said. "And a man of your age, having done the things you've done. I see rather bloody days ahead for you. Pain and humiliation at the hands of lesser men than. I suspect you'll be spending many years cursing me for not ending you tonight."

"But, your fathers...can't they...?," Remus said, desperate for the The Favored Son not to be saying what he was saying.

"No," The Son said. "I'm afraid it's in our best interests to terminate our relationship. There are more important things that need our attention right now, as I'm sure you know."

"I see," Remus whispered. Thirty years. He had given The Fathers thirty loyal years. He had committed unspeakable sins for them and the future they had promised. And, just like that, he was nothing to them.

"However," The Son said, "I can offer you one option."

With that, The Son tossed something into the cell. It landed at Remus' feet. He looked down to see a belt. His belt. The belt they'd taken from him, along with his shoelaces, before placing him alone in the cell.

"I see," Remus said, barely audible even to himself. This was the final humiliation, after all he had done for them. This was all he was worth to them.

"Consider that one last favor from My Fathers," The Son said.

With that, as uneventfully as it had opened, the cell door closed.

To Be Continued...

THE **Outside World**

If you've enjoyed this series and would like to see it continue, please let me know by leaving a rating on Amazon and/or Goodreads.

ALSO BY THE AUTHOR

MODUS OPERANDI: A TECH-NOIR MYSTERY

"Amnitol: Take a vacation from yourself."

In the not-to-distant future, as the world recovers from a cataclysmic event, Harvard Wilcox has erased his own memory. He isn't welcome anywhere he goes, and it isn't long before gangsters, cops, and shady corporate agents are chasing him down. With no idea how he'd gotten himself into this, he certainly doesn't know how he'll get himself out.

ABOUT THE AUTHOR

Jonathan was born and raised in the real-life Landfall: Portland, Oregon. When he's not writing, he's working in service and administration all over the country. Mostly, he's worked the night shift for six different hotels over 15 years, which has inspired far more Fantasy/Sci-Fi stories than it should.

www.ingramcontent.com/pod-product-compliance
Lightning Source LLC
Chambersburg PA
CBHW032126170626
46808CB00006B/2122